Thou Worm Jacob

THOU WORM
JACOB

MARK MIRSKY

The Macmillan Company, New York
Collier-Macmillan Ltd., London

Second Printing 1967
The Macmillan Company, New York
Collier-Macmillan Canada Ltd., Toronto, Ontario

Printed in the United States of America

FOR THE HON. WILFRED S. MIRSKY

Contents

Fear not, thou worm Jacob
                    ISAIAH, 41:14

The Family of Jacob
weak
like the worm,
its strength only
in its mouth
    COMMENTARY OF RASHI,
    ELEVENTH CENTURY

Introduction

I'VE GOT the whole state of Jewish affairs right between my fingers!

What? You don't understand? Take a seat. Don't worry, it won't break. A bit cracked but it's had a rest. Watch out! Watch out for that pile of books. Knock one over, my whole place is on your head. Pages, dust, dirty yarmulkes. Eh! Let it fall.

You see these hands? With these hands, I, Bissel, in the old days used to bind mighty books. Rashi and Maimonides I stitched two feet deep just in their indexes. Glue by the potfuls I poured into the backs of Babylonian Talmuds. I wrestled with the stiff covers of Ibn Ezra. Judah ha-Levi and his delicate sheaves I spun into fine brown calf. And when I was finished?

When an old siddur that had come in rusting with age, its leaves falling apart, worms hanging out like bookmarks, when it lay before me bound between stiff board and cloth as tight as Noah in his ark, its pages crackling like parchment, I could weep. The title I laid on in gilt heavier than the gold oil of the menorah candle. To me, it was a commandment to restore it to its family. I dwelt among the deeds of Judah the Prince. I carried on the work of the great Gamaliel. The

1

Gaons of Vilna were dependent on me. In those days it was a pleasure to bind a book.

And now? It's a laugh. What I bind for the Jews, my father wouldn't have used for his outhouse. I am ashamed to look between the covers. *What's Jewish about Being Jewish?* by Professor Haman Rosenberg; *The Disintegration of Jewish Suburbia* by Endelbum the Episcopalian; *Let's Give Up!* by Rabbi Harold Himmelfarb; *Don't Kick a Dead Dog*—Mendele Weepe.

All right, I'm joking. But you think I'm kidding? Pretty soon it will be worse.

You are smiling at me. Oooooh, you got a dirty smile on your lips. Something is under your tongue, a little poison. You got a big question to ask. From a strictly objective point of view and for the sake of any stranger listening, you have to submit a Shyla—why?

Why? Why not? Why not let our community go to pot. Why be Jewish?

You think I'm going to answer you? Well . . . I'll answer you. Like they answer the ignorant son, I'll answer you. I'll tell you a story.

It's an old tale from long ago when things were worse than they are now. Did you ever hear of Putchnik— Greater Putchnik of little Russia? No? Well, not many people did. In fact, only a little while after it was founded, more and more heard less and less. Pretty soon the number included the whole world. And it heard nothing.

First, the merchants forgot about it. Because the

tributary it was on dried up and its trade had never been more than a few dried potatoes anyway. Then a forest sprung up on one side and a swamp sunk into the earth on the other. So the tsar didn't bother with it. Finally, a pogrom removed all the Jews from that part of Russia and even the Jewish Charity Board rubbed it off the books.

But Putchnik endured. You might even say Putchnik prospered. Flowers sprouted under the benches of the synagogue. Wheat rustled down the main street. After two hundred years the adult Jewish male population jumped from nineteen to twenty and the town seriously debated building another temple to accommodate the second minyan.

That was the year of the Catastrophe. For, just as the number reached twenty . . . bang! Just like that it went right down to nineteen again.

What happened? Did someone leave? Not exactly. Someone came by. To Putchnik? Who knew about Putchnik? One night a chilly wind blew through town. In the morning, people realized they had a visitor. An ashman. A collector of rags and bones. But Death was not fair and square with the town of Putchnik. It was not content to humble the pride of the village by taking off one of its male members at random. It snatched the only son of the Rabbi in the bargain.

Yes, in that year the last issue of the rabbinical family in Putchnik died and when his father quickly followed him, the town had to elect a new Rabbi. A post that had been passed down by inheritance for two hundred years was thrown open to election.

What an election! There was only one man in town who could read, so he was elected. Not that I do not value Rabbi Loisel and his descendants. That excellent man was a real scholar. He knew his Torah by heart and the Talmud was on the back of his hand. Only it was a little unfortunate that he should be deaf.

Yes, it was in that miserable little defect, really a trifle, that the troubles of Putchnik began.

It was in the year of this election that the world stopped hearing from Putchnik. You see, since the new Rabbi couldn't hear anything, he wasn't interested in listening to the world. And as the world had never listened to Putchnik . . . things were impossible.

But Rabbi Loisel's defect had more serious consequences. Naturally, the Rabbi couldn't sing very well. The reading of the Torah had to be carried on by those who couldn't read. And in the second generation after Loisel, even that delight passed out of the synagogue. For it was the task of the Rabbi to teach the young the chant. Metrically, these new singers were perfect. They knew only one note. The descendants of the first Rabbi Loisel were also deaf. In the first generation the service in the synagogue was unpleasant. In the second it was burdensome. By the third—why strain the imagination, you never heard it, and be thankful.

Moreover, a deaf man sees things differently, so to speak. The Rabbis Loisel looked at things in a strange way. They saw with a hard gaze the world before them and their observations sharpened. For, as the post passed down from father to son, there grew up a tradition that the Rabbi Loisel would refuse to credit anything he did not see with his own eyes. Our forefathers demanded a golden calf. Rabbi Loisel asked for facts and figures.

The songs of the Torah were forgotten. Its promises seemed foolish. Its hopes, unfounded. The town of Putchnik believed what it could see. Could it see the Messiah? No! It couldn't even smell him. What could Putchnik see? Putchnik could see Putchnik. So Putchnik believed in what it could see. And Putchnik looked terrible.

Thus for the next two hundred years were the people of Putchnik miserable.

And the Rabbis Loisel? The sound of our people's prophecy was a dead letter to their eyes. The Bible was a scroll without vowels. Under their scrutiny the streams of Zion dried up surer than the lost tributary of Putchnik. They were interested in the measurements of the temple. Israel's census obsessed them. Nothing else, however, seemed to matter.

Thus, for the next two hundred years, the Rabbis Loisel lectured each Sabbath on the measurements of the temple and Israel's census.

> Sing, O Heavens: and be joyful,
> O Earth: And break forth into
> singing, O Mountains: for the
> Lord Hath Comforted His People
> and will have mercy upon His
> afflicted. (Isaiah)

After two hundred years a stranger was seen in Putchnik. Late one afternoon, on the outskirts of town, he appeared, where the swamp crept into the forest, a

young man robed in rags of strange colors and Bedouin
stripes, proceeding along the dry riverbed which led
through surrounding hills to the village. He pushed
slowly, almost blindly, down the weed-choked road, his
staff gliding like a sword through the briars. The
shepherd dogs, for two centuries as silent and sullen as
their masters, sent up a delighted howling and Putchnik's flock of sheep began to bleat. Their pastor flung
his crook aside and ran toward the village, mouthing
the news to the dumb hills. It was the Sabbath and,
except for the shepherd, all the Jews of Putchnik were
gathered in the synagogue.

You may have guessed that the Sabbath was not a
day of joy in Putchnik. The nineteen adult male Jews
assembled out of obligation rather than inclination.
Children had been excused from the ordeal and the
women came only to keep their husbands company.
The Rabbi Loisel refused to show up until six in the
evening, which was the time set aside for his sermon.
The rest he left to the member appointed to chant the
Law. As you know, this reader couldn't read and only
knew one note. The pace of life in Putchnik was usually
unbearably dull. On the Sabbath it became excruciat-
ing.

Some of the members of the congregation slept
through the service. Others pulled the hairs from their
beards with nervousness. A few hid in the corners and
wept with the boredom. Occasionally they all moaned
together to keep up the spirits of the chanter.

Into this desolate room burst the shepherd. The
heavy wooden door slammed behind him. Up and

down he jumped on the synagogue benches, flailing his arms. He fell to the floor and beat the boards with his fists. The poor man was a mute.

"Mad?" wondered the congregation, gathering around the writhing body. They dumped a bucket of ice water in his face. The mute gnashed his teeth. He tried to spit his words at them. Such carrying on is not seemly in a synagogue. So they seized his legs and began to drag him toward the door.

At that moment a crash was heard on the threshold. The congregation stopped. They listened. A hand was groping on the iron handle of the synagogue door. With a squeal, it was flung open.

For a second a young man stood under the lintel. Then he staggered across the back of the room and up the aisle. Stumbling against the bottom step of the bema, he began to climb the stairs. Amazed, the chanter looked down at him, the scrolls half lifted from the reading table in surprise. He put out his hand to stop the stranger, but his arms were seized and he rose into the air. As the old reader opened his mouth to protest, he was let go. The floor smacked him in the face and he tumbled along the boards. Above him, on the platform, the stranger hitched his dusty robes upon bulky shoulders like the folds of a prayer shawl and lifted his face to the astounded congregation.

His lips were a knot of scarlet threads. Turning the parchment scrolls until they were tight against one another, he folded the pillar of the Law into his bosom and bound his arms tight around it. Two holes sunk into his face. Shafts into darkness, deep and black.

Under the stranger's unblinking gaze the congregation trembled. He moved his hands to speak; they seemed to sparkle with rings, and his limbs to be set in sockets of gold. Crimson, his lips parted. And a voice arose like a whisper out of the dust.

> And you shall be brought down
> and shall speak out of the ground
> and your speech shall be low
> out of the dust.

Never before had they heard the Hebrew sung. The sound of the Law had been indeed but a whisper. The melody of the Bible was so soft and melancholy in the singer's mouth that their courage grew faint. The spirit of the members dispersed. It was blown and driven like chaff before the slight breath of the chanter.

> Drunken, but not with wine; they stagger
> but not from beer.

> For the Lord has poured out upon you
> the spirit of deep sleep,
> closed your eyes: and the eyes of your rulers,
> the seers, has he covered.

> And the vision of all becomes to you
> the words of a book that is sealed.
> Men deliver it to one that is learned,
> saying, read this, please; and he says,
> I cannot; for it is sealed.

The song rang out.

> And the book is delivered to him
> that is not learned, saying, read this, please,
> and he says, I am ignorant.

The old reader, sprawled on the floor, pushed his nose into the dirt. Ashamed, the congregation bowed their heads and pulled their shoulders together, rocking back and forth in woe.

> Therefore the Lord said, Since
> this people draw near me with their mouth,
> and with their lips do honor me, but
> have removed their heart far
> from me, and their fear toward me
> is taught by the precept of men.

And the voice lifted itself high and nasal, oppressing them with sarcasm.

> I will do a wonder! A marvel!
> The wisdom of their wise men shall perish,
> the understanding of their prudent men be hid.

Then grasping the Law, the singer fell across the lectern of the synagogue and cried in a bitter voice.

> Therefore my loins are filled with pain;
> like the pains of a pregnant woman.
> I was bowed down at the hearing of it.
> I was dismayed at the sight of it.

The Jews winced and squirmed on the benches. They pulled at their prayer shawls and twisted the cotton fringes in their fingers.

> We have been with child, we have been
> with pain, and we have brought forth wind.
> We have delivered no help on this earth.

The congregation fell upon its face. Its nose smashed in blood. Its eyes winced in pain. It stretched forth its tongue on the boards, tasted dirt and vomit. It turned upon itself and tore at its clothes. Maddened, it bit the flesh of its arm.

> Howl ye: for the day of the Lord
> is at hand.

Then the singer rose to his full height and cried above them like a trumpet.

> Behold, the name of the Lord comes
> from afar, burning with anger, heavy
> with burden. His lips are full of fury.
> His tongue is a fire that devours.

The stranger's lips trembled with purple. His tongue bled. He reached his hand out over the congregation so that its jaw distended and its mouth gaped.

> There shall be a bridle in the jaws of
> the people causing them to err.

The congregation writhed on the floorboards. The stranger shouted like brass choked with spit. "Conceive chaff!" The congregation clutched at its windpipe, gasping with flushed face. "Bring forth stubble!" And its lung twisted tight as a rag. "Your breath as fire, devour you!"

The figure of the young man mounted the west wall of the synagogue, a black shadow writhing among the shapes of the setting sun. The shadow of a breath, the Law echoed, in a whisper from the wall, over the congregation doubled in agony, staring . . .

> Sing, O barren, you that did not
> bear.

It began to wail through the lifeless empty room, ". . . for more are the children of the desolate than the children of the married man." The sound wound through the open synagogue door out into the desolate streets of the abandoned little town. It echoed down the narrow muddy alleys of Putchnik and over the thatched rooftops of its hovels. It was carried beyond the hills, the swamp and the forest. Imperceptible with the wind, it wailed over the wide empty spaces of Russia and the world.

> Enlarge the place of your tent,
> let them stretch forth the curtains
> of your house, spare not, lengthen
> your cords, strengthen the stakes.
>
> For you will break forth on the right
> hand and on the left; and your seed shall
> inherit the Gentiles; and desolate cities
> will they revive.

The sun, as it sank behind the mountains, shot through the doorway with a brilliant scarlet flame. It caught the garments of the singer and set them ablaze. Robed in fire, he cried from the altar.

> Fear not: thy Maker is thine husband.

All the room blazed without a sound. The singer turned, turned on the platform upward in his flaming robes, the Law cradled to his breast, the congregation gaping into the light. A sweetness turned inside him, until tears broke out on his cheeks, and he heard . . .

> For a small moment I have forsaken thee
> but with great mercies I will gather thee.

Small and still, the voice whispered in the silence of the synagogue. All was quiet. The sun had crept into the cradle of the hills. The last flames flickered from the young man's shawl and were extinguished. Through the door the cool breeze of evening rushed with pale breath. It rustled the fringes of the congregation's prayer shawl. Over the stiff body the singer bent and stretched out his hands, "Comfort you, comfort you, my people." And the congregation stirred in his arms.

> Every valley shall be exalted, and every
> mountain and hill shall be made low; and
> the crooked shall be made straight.
>
> And the glory of the Lord shall be revealed,
> and all flesh shall see it together.

And the singer sang, "Cry!" And the congregation spoke: "What shall I cry? All flesh is grass, and all the goodliness thereof is as the flower of the field." It sang in a hollow voice. "The grass withers, the flower fades: because the spirit of the Lord blows upon it: surely the people is grass." Then sang the singer to the congregation in his arms, "The grass withers, the flower fades, but the word of our God shall stand forever."

He clasped the congregation to him. "Lift up your voice with strength," he whispered by its wan cheek. And asked,

> Who has directed the spirit of the Lord,
> or being his counsellor has taught him?

The question smoldered like a brand in the ear of the congregation. The stranger's lips were the blue fever of coals.

> To whom then will you liken God?
> What likeness will you compare him to?

Furious, the singer shook the form of the congregation. "Have you not known? Have you not heard?" He dug his fingers into its shoulder blade. "Has it not been told you from the beginning?" He arose with it, grappling. "Have you not understood from the foundations of the earth?"

> It is he that sits upon the circle of
> the earth, and the inhabitants of it are
> as grasshoppers.

And he flung it to the ground with a shout.

> To whom then will you liken me, or shall
> I be equal? says the Holy One.

> Lift up your eyes on high, and see
> Who has created all this?

The congregation turned and groaned on the floor. The limbs of every man ached. Dust sealed their eyes. In each throat thirst seared like a dry flame. The singer flung himself into their midst, grasping the heavy candelabrum of the altar. His right hand gripped the Law to his breast. The huge silver candle holders shone and glinted, burning bushes in the dark pit of the synagogue. The eyes of the Jews blinked in the diamonds of brilliant light. Uncertain, they stumbled to their feet. Through the room the stranger flung candles from the blazing branch of the menorah. The hot wax dripped upon their fingers. It stung the flesh of their hands. Yet they saw each other for the first time. As strangers find themselves kin. As with burning face, Joseph beheld his brother Benjamin. Light struck them. Each man fell upon his fellow's neck, speechless with joy. Into his cousin's arms he wound himself and danced with happiness. Shoulder linked to shoulder and candles flaming, the Jews circled the singer. He turned in their midst, clasping the Law and the fiery candlestick.

> I have a long time held my peace:
> I have been still, and refrained myself;
> now will I cry like a travailing woman;
> I will gasp and pant at once.

The heaviness of two hundred years fell away from their throats. They remembered the melody. They raised their voices with him. They sang together in the voice of the Lord. The cry of destruction was their covenant. It smoked in the nostril as a sacrifice. It was their prophecy and cloyed upon the tongue as honey.

> I will make waste mountains and hills,
> and dry up all their herbs; make rivers
> islands, dry up the pools.

Faster and faster the congregation danced. Candles guttered in the swaying hands. Again and again their heavy limbs were lifted into the air. The press of groaning, shouting men jumped up and then came crashing down. The floors buckled under the tread. The boards cracked, then splintered as the hobnailed boots tore grooves deeper than script into the wood. Higher and higher they bounded, laughing and screaming. The song, like wine, rose and fell in their throats with each effort. Arm twisted about arm as they whirled themselves round with drunken fervor. Sweat streamed in channels from each brow. Body jarred into body. The liquor of one another's smell was hot upon them and in the warmth of the rhythm they were spinning like a single limb about the singer.

An arm of God, the circle rippled around him. And as they danced, the ceiling fell away. They leapt into the sky and danced over the whole world.

> And I will bring thee blind by a way
> that they knew not: I will lead them
> in paths that they have not known. I
> will make darkness light before them
> and crooked things straight.

Here they skipped, jeering at themselves with laughter and with joy.

> They shall be turned back, they shall be
> greatly ashamed, that trust in graven images,
> that say to the molten images, You are our gods.

And the stranger? He spun a black die against the heavens. His eyes strained into the blank expanse of the skies.

> Who is blind but my servant? Who is blind
> as he that is perfect, and blind as the Lord's
> servant?

At this moment Rabbi Loisel stepped through the synagogue door. He looked before him in amazement. His congregation was leaping about like so many he-goats. Somebody was up in the air with the Torah scrolls.

"What's going on!" he shouted. "What are you carrying on for? What is there to jump for?"

His eyes searched through the dark room, the mass of flashing shapes and flickering candles, for rhyme or reason. He shrieked so high his ears popped. "See what you're doing? Now in the air, now on the ground. You'll break your necks! For what? Explain! What?"

But his piping, toneless voice was hopelessly lost in the deafening chant of the congregation. Rabbi Loisel walked back to the door, yet once again he looked at the wild dancing herd. He could not believe his eyes. "Don't you see what you are doing?" He stood on his tiptoes. "Don't you seeeeeee . . ." he screamed till his throat gave out. "Your heels are on the ceiling! You're on each other's necks. You are kissing with the lips. You're dancing? For what? You are in each other's arms? For *what?*"

His congregation was a thousand leagues away. High as a kite, coattails flapping over the Universe. Divine Presence was upon them.

Rabbi Loisel pulled on his ears with anger. He cried from the door, "And it's all in such bad taste."

A speck on the earth. A mote of dust. Naturally the congregation ignored him. As the door slammed, they encircled the sun. Did the singer notice him?

Why should he? How could he? What a question! The singer was blind.

Blind as a bat! What do you make of that, eh? Better close your eyes and listen. If you can. If not, tell you what. Why look on with a sour puss? You'll just upset me. Get up!

Right! Right! Go home. The world is full of good books on geometry, folders of maps and charts, boxes of IBM cards. Settle down somewhere and enjoy yourself. Zei gesund!

. To be
frank, the last of its kind. Where are you going to get
such stories in Dorchester? In the delicatessens of Blue
Hill Avenue? Only the prices leap to the sky. Do miracles occur? Where? In baloney sandwiches between
slices of rye? Do they? Know of any?

Oooooh listen! Get ready to swallow a mouthful.

CHAPTER I

The Left-Handed
Moyhel

SO DREIZEN the left-handed Moyhel was walking down Blue Hill Avenue, bemoaning the fate of the Jews.

The moans had begun at exactly two o'clock P.M. time. Dreizen had come down the creaking hall stairs of 11 Mclellan Street, finagled with the broken latch of the mail receptacle, and had discovered that his relief check had not arrived.

"To make an old man with a bad leg come down all these stairs for nothing?" Dreizen asked of the vacant box.

"An old man . . . a bad leg . . . all these stairs," Dreizen repeated. He raised his voice above a mumble and addressed himself to the ear of Mrs. Shwartz's broken window on the first floor of 11 Mclellan Street. (It was deaf. The bottom floor was tenantless. Mrs. Shwartz and family had departed for Brookline, leaving the neighborhood at the mercy of the Goyim and the Shvartzas.)

"For nothing?" the left-handed Moyhel asked. His face puckered in ingenuous amazement. He knocked softly upon the cracked black paint of the mailbox. A flake fell from the blistering old enamel. Dreizen poked his finger inside. Dust wept into the wrinkles of his fingertip.

Up and down flicked the Moyhel's fingernail, searching for an envelope. Nothing. He waited.

Perhaps Mrs. Shwartz would stick her head out the broken window and give him the check. He waited some more.

And then he waited until his forefinger had trembled across the bottom and along the sides and into all the corners of the post office's receptacle. And he was still waiting as he turned and hobbled down the porch stairs, crossing the street to see if the mailbox of Jones the Shvartza was full. Perhaps the mailman had forgotten Harvard Street. Nu, who could tell with the post office full of lazy Irish Goyim. Maybe, Mr. Postman didn't come already. All right, so he would wait. He would wait for the mail.

A sheaf of brightly colored notices and glittering white letters shone from the Negro's mailbox. Neither friend nor department store nor politician nor bill collector forgot Jones. His mailbox intercepted the tides of the city. He dwelt in the bosom and at the crossroads of its life.

So it was with a heart heavy with the weight of shattered expectations that Dreizen, the left-handed one, made his way to where the shady old elms of Mclellan Street gave way to the bare concrete lamppost of Blue Hill Avenue. It was with a mind not insensible to the indignity that he turned the corner.

The Goyim were attempting to cut him off from sustenance. He saw them sifting his letter from the Government out of the mail sacks. They were laughing. Dreizen? Dreizen? Dreizen from Mclellan Street don't need no relief check. Cross out the name and give it to Jones. Jones? You know . . . Jones the Shvartza.

The tongue of the Moyhel was bitter with the salt of Fate. His heart rattled the apple in his throat. Aching teeth bit his lips in pain. Tears wet his eyes. What kind of a world was this?

And it was at this moment of personal distress that the soul of Dreizen, transcending its own acute bereavement, cried out for Israel. It left the familiar chambers of its own complaints, rose into the Heavens, and espoused the indignities and bereavements of a people. In front of the Everlasting Doors a left-handed Moyhel moaned for the fate of the Jews.

There is a saying somewhere in the Talmud.

Deep, somewhere in the Talmud . . . I forget.

Wait! I remember. Sifre Num. Pinehas. Rabbi Nathan—"God does not reject the prayer of the multitude." Wherefore, we can infer, if a soul cries out in its own distress, the ear of the Holy One, blessed be He, is deaf; but if it cry forth in the distress of another, the hearing is A-1 letter perfect. Imagine, then, when Dreizen the left-handed Moyhel called forth in the name of the Almighty One's favorites, the Jewish people, the Children of Israel.

Perhaps in Heaven . . . drums rolled, trumpets blared, Gabriel the winged one blew a mighty Trooo-oh on the shofar. But on Blue Hill Avenue the M.T.A. bus honked its horn, and God's delegate to Earth, Insoft the

Cantor from Havana, leaned his head out the window and called:

"Stop. Yooh, Dreizen. Wait a minute, I'll walk down with you."

And Dreizen stopped.

But as the bus did *not* stop but rolled on to its appointed assignation at the Esmond Street landing, one could hear the high-pitched shrieking of the Holy One's appointed deputy crying out:

"Stop, Mr. Bus. Stop, Driver. You missed a stop. Emergency! Stop! It don't stop at Mclellan Street? Why? Something wrong mit Mclellan? Stop. Something wrong mit you? Oy stop quick. You ran over an old lady. Stop. It's an emergency. You gonna make an old man walk all the way back from Esmond to Mclellan Street? I got rights. Back. To do this to an old man. Oy, a klog. You a devil . . ."

The driver, a red-jowled, emerald-eyed ward of St. Patrick's, kept his countenance. The bus reached Esmond Street. Insoft, the Cantor from Havana, limped down the stairs. On the last step of the landing he turned and addressed the driver. Tilting his head with its little black yarmulke to the side, he said in an aggrieved and mournful yet distinct voice:

"What you are? An anti-Semite!"

Oy. A bus full of ancient Jewish ladies from Dorchester and Mattapan echoed the sentiment. A low but fearful Oy shuddered down the aisles and shook the walls of the Metropolitan Transit Authority's vehicle before the driver could shut the door on the old man and drown his conscience in the silent onrush of the engine.

OY

On Blue Hill Avenue, halfway between Mclellan and Esmond streets, Dreizen the Moyhel and Insoft the Cantor embraced.

"A Tragedy," the Moyhel murmured softly into Insoft's ear, preparing to elaborate.

"Disgrace," shrieked Insoft, interrupting him. It was the voice of a frantic jay. He pulled back to address the Moyhel, his arms beat the air, his pitch cracked. It shattered into grace notes. "A MAJOR DIS*grace* . . . Dis*grace* . . . Dis*grace* . . . Dis*grace*," the Cantor sang up and down, whistling the last syllable with vociferous relish through his broken front teeth; and brandished his finger at two female shoppers.

The sisters Shwartzekoff, Bella and Rosie, sixty-year-old grand dames of Dorchester, were returning home from Katz's Kosher Supermarket by the G&G. Their bosoms were laden with groceries and their arms outstretched around huge shopping bags. In the suffocating embrace of their swollen pink flesh, packages of schmaltz herring and raw beefsteak oozed a rancid and tantalizing perfume which dripped from the bottom of the paper bags onto the pavement under their feet. Here in the shade of the Shwartzekoffs' trembling hams, under the shifting mountains of sagging flesh, a retinue of hungry flies buzzed up and down, devouring the salty nectar.

Rosie, with the 3-D chins, listed to the right side

under the weight of the beefsteak and herring; the jars of kosher gherkins, the cabbages, horseradish . . . the variegated multitude of kuchen. (Although on the left she bore up bravely the stowage of a dozen of grapefruit, oranges, bananas, figs, dates, pomegranates and coconuts; also tomatoes and onions, while a pennant of beet tops snapped smartly in the Blue Hill Avenue breeze.)

Bella, older by an hour (they were twins) though similarly cargoed, carried her tonnage with a more sprightly carriage; and supported the loaves of pumpernickel and bushels of potatoes with an almost demure gait as she rolled from side to side with bottles of Geritol and barbecued carcasses of eighteen-pound turkeys.

The flagships were arrested in their heaving and ineluctable movement up Blue Hill Avenue by the cry and crack of Insoft's cantorial voice. They were becalmed as the forefinger of the Cantor from Havana, shaking its bone, descended upon them.

"A disgrace."

A lunatic sun glared in the hollows of Insoft's eyes. It leapt like a flame from his lean finger to accuse these women of obesity; to testify to the guilt of their sloth; to indict them for gluttony; to draw to their attention that Jews were going hungry before them.

The sisters Shwartzekoff drew their parcels in as best they could between the tremulous hollows of their breasts. They would defend their sustenance.

"A Major Disgrace . . ." the voice of Insoft was rising high; higher than even the soprano robin dreams of in drunken lilac boughs amid the nights of May. It was passing high into the ethereal region above falsetto. For the smells of food were maddening Insoft. The scent of schmaltz herring rose into his wasted and crooked body to inspire him. Once more he was the grosse Chazzen of Havana. Upward he stretched on his one good leg. Twitch . . . His nose began to twitch, going crazy with the fragrance of freshly baked pumpernickel and just-barbecued turkey. His head was shaking. The fumes of kosher gherkins careened in his brain.

"A disgrace . . . the Jewish people . . ." and his voice broke completely. Through his throat the wind rushed as through hollow reeds. It made no sound except to rustle the Cantor's larynx sweetly.

The Holy One, blessed be He, has eloquence. He filled with ease five books of the Tanach. His breath turned over mountains and made them skip like rams. That voice resounds like a clap of thunder. It rumbles beneath the earthquake; roars within the volcano. But when His cantors, the singers of His praise, the psalmists of His glory, grow old, where is it?

Sometimes Silence is Golden.

As Insoft's voice broke and left his throat, he gasped and caught his breath. The air that filled his shriveled belly was full of the goodness of life. It drew in through famished nostrils the smells that the Almighty, in infinite mercy, has ordained for the comfort of man. Tears started in the Chazzen's eyes. His foot came back to earth. His body almost crumpled with pleasure to the pavement.

Among our people they say that to a threat the heart

of man will grow stiff and invulnerable, but to a tear it must bow without defense. Is this true of a woman? Looking down over the stricken Cantor, the hearts of the sisters Shwartzekoff sagged.

Dreizen leaned forward to support his friend. He looked up at the women. In a phrase that indicated the Universe, Dreizen wailed, "He's a Chazzen."

"A Chazzen?" the women asked.

"A Chazzen," Dreizen the left-handed Moyhel replied, his voice slow and sad.

"A Chazzen," the women repeated, shaking their sympathetic chins. That the Jews could reduce their Chazzens to such a state of impoverishment. It was not to be believed. How had it happened? At one time a Chazzen did not dare to be abroad at such a time of day for fear of being kidnapped by the President and Board of some outlying suburban Synagogue. At twelve noon there was a press of Jews so thick on the Avenue that the Chassidim had to beware of being smothered in their beards. But if a Chazzen should chance to walk amid the crowd, lo and behold they cleared an aisle for him so quickly and respectfully. You would imagine the high priest Aaron himself was on his way to the G&G for a corned-beef sandwich.

And now on Blue Hill Avenue, formerly the hub of New England Judaism, a Chazzen fainted from hunger. A Comment. A Parable! Dreizen and the two women intoned in chorus, "A Chazzen."

Miracles will occur. The voice of Insoft, Cantor from Havana, returned. "A Chazzen," he rasped in response, blinking a beautiful and pathetic smile at the sisters Shwartzekoff. "I was, used to be, a Chazzen."

"And what a Chazzen." The Moyhel added the strophe. "Rosenblatt with all his reputation wouldn't sing in the same town as Insoft on High Holidays. Used to be Mr. Insoft here was chief Cantor of Havana."

The women looked with wonder on Insoft. He acknowledged modestly, shaking his head with the sad pride of those who have known the reversal of great fortunes. "Look at me. A Chazzen? Used to be. Stones! I'm singing to them. Mount Olive Cemetery. Rosh Hashanah—a job. I get it. Twenty Jews. I sing to them, at the schul in Rosindale. For twenty Jews, listen, Rosindale don't deserve no Chazzen."

The Shwartzekoff sisters sighed their condolence. Didn't they know? Weren't they members of the Sisterhood of Congregation Bas-Sheva? It was a business proposition to get anybody to bake a cookie. Do you think Jews paid any attention to religious obligations? Wasn't it always they who were imposed upon to make the gefilte fish? And supply the herring for Hadassah luncheons? Believe me, someday the plates were going to be empty at one of those brunches.

Insoft had allowed a strategic pause. Now he began slowly and softly a chant as heart-rending and melancholy as the solemn and awesome Kol Nidre itself.

"A terrible thing . . . All day . . . I'm sitting at Mount Olive. For what? Come out, Jews! Pay respect to parents! I'm waiting. I'm waiting. All morning I'm waiting. One Jew. One Jew does show up to do his father's grave an honor. All morning I wait to say an El Rachamim.

Even a finiff, do I make it? Today, five-dollar bills are not growing on graves. Used to be, even in slow season, used to be I could afford now and then in my mouth to put a cough drop. The cemetery cares? Oh yeh! A favor they're doing—letting an old man stand all day under the sun?"

Insoft stopped to breathe and began anew in a voice vibrating with a splendor that only the great Pinchick has known in our time. "Today, showed up one Jew. I told him, I'm going to say such an El Rachamim. Your father's stone will weep. What he tells me, you know? What he says, you know? 'Never mind.' Never mind? 'Never mind, I'm an atheist.' An atheist? Dreizen? Are the atheists going to support the Chazzens?"

Dreizen shook his head slowly with restrained grief. It was only too clear. It was but a matter of time. The Moyhels too would be cut off.

Insoft turned to the sisters Shwartzekoff. He asked timidly of them, as if half-expecting a reply in the affirmative, "An atheist . . . maybe you?"

"Heaven forbid. I should be an atheist?" exclaimed Rosie. Bella mumbled amen.

"A gantse maiseh, you're not an atheist," Insoft replied. "Because the state of the Jews"—he waved his arms—"eeh . . . ehh . . . a terrible thing!"

"A terrible thing." Bella smiled back in toothless agreement.

"Terrible," echoed Rosie, opening a mouth full of battered gold.

Insoft sniffed the air redolent with barbecued turkey as if to give them their next cue. His congregation, however, was untrained. An awkward pause resulted. Insoft sniffed again and, closing his eyes, tilted his head back and forth to signify that the essence of something divine was in the air.

"A beautyfulled day," Bella tried.

"Beautyfulled?" Rosie essayed.

Insoft snorted. Pride would not allow him to pursue a handout directly, but the smell of the barbecued turkey could drive him mad in another moment. Dreizen interposed. In that soft and sad voice of his, but this time with just a (the merest) touch of banter, he remarked, "Mmmm . . . A wonderful-smelling turkey you got there. You cooked it yourself?"

"It's a ready-made," Bella replied with pride. "A barbecued from the supermarket."

"Kosher?" the Moyhel asked, as if in doubt that such a miracle could be possible.

"Kosher," Rosie rejoined with enthusiasm.

"Kosher turkeys? Ready-made? Insoft, do you hear? A kosher barbecued turkey."

Insoft nodded his head, stunned with joy. It was a revelation. Together he and Dreizen sniffed the air before them, then exclaimed as if they could already taste the miracle, "Mmmm . . ."

Rosie smelt a cue. She drew her parcels under the obtruding battlements of women. Sourly she whispered, "You wouldn't like."

"Fattening," Bella rumbled omnisciently. Her share of the greasy brown-paper bags nestled securely between swelling turrets.

Dreizen and Insoft regarded the two citadels of Zion.

A direct assault was impossible. Only the guile of Jacob followed by a quick strategy of Joshua would snatch the victory. On a golden turkey wing protruding from one of Bella's shopping bags, Insoft fixed a terrible eye. He shook his head disapprovingly. Solemnly Dreizen sighed through his nose.

Bella and Rosie observed this behavior with suspicion. The sisters wrinkled their numerous brows. Finally Bella asked nonchalantly, "So what's the matter?"

Insoft and Dreizen ignored her question. The former whispered loudly into the latter's ear, "Kosher? A turkey? It don't smell like."

The latter shouted softly into the former's ear, "It don't *look* too kosher neither." Then both former and latter began to daven, rocking back and forth, their eyes intent with piety upon the sidewalk.

The sisters Shwartzekoff stared at each other. The embattled resolution was shaken. After all, a Cantor and a Moyhel know what is and isn't kosher. It was vaguely unholy, feasting all afternoon before the television screen. Perhaps it was sacrilegious to nash upon the crisp legs and wings of a ready-made. Maybe they ought to propitiate the religious authorities. Bella began, "Would you try . . . ?"

"An experiment!" Insoft cut in sternly. He would not allow her to finish.

"Experiment!" the sisters Shwartzekoff urged meekly.

Bella slowly removed a fligel from the barbecued turkey at the top of her bag. With ponderous ceremony she awarded it to him. The turkey wing melted in his mouth like a fat bullock on the high flame of the altar.

Smacking his lips, Insoft complimented. "Mr. Dreizen, you should experiment a fligel like this."

The sisters Shwartzekoff began to back away, terrified. On tiptoes Insoft and Dreizen beamed at them. The Moyhel extended his trembling fingers into Bella's bag. He stripped the turkey of its other fligel with all the professional delicacy of his calling. "I wonder . . ." Insoft began to intone as the Moyhel with his withered tooth stumps broke into the bones of roasted fligel even to the marrow, "I wonder"—a benign smile wetted the grease upon the Cantor's lips—"what should the *breast* of a kosher barbecued turkey *test* like . . . ?"

It is written that the needy shall not want. Nor shall the belly of the righteous go hungry. In a matter of minutes Dreizen and Insoft lightened the burden of the sisters Shwartzekoff by two barbecued turkeys, a jar of kosher gherkins, half a loaf of pumpernickel, assorted fruits. And the bones of three schmaltz herring lay prostrate upon the pavement, picked so clean they were not even fit carrion for the flies.

"I smell a schmaltza!" Insoft was singing. His nose was in a jar of pickled herring and sour cream.

Kashruth to the winds! Health overrules all laws. Rosie couldn't believe it. Her food! Her nourishment! And sacrilege! She screamed. Hysterical, she pulled a bleeding beefsteak from her bag. She slammed the Cantor in the Face. He gagged on a herring and began to cough sour cream.

Don't laugh. Were you never invited to dances? Did you come home to nibble on chicken bones, turkey drumsticks, a shank of lamb? Did you have to bury your heart in the holes of bagels, in egg rolls, bialys, and loaves of dark pumpernickel? Rosie was betrothed to food. The Cantor and the Moyhel snatched away her beloved.

And Bella? She was bigger than Rosie. Bella's eyes were wide, a wanderer in delirium. What were they eating? Her life! She cried. She pulled a stalk of bananas out and pounded Dreizen on the head. The bottle of Geritol slipped from the Moyhel's lips. It crashed to the pavement. A limpid stream of liquid revitalizer gurgled irrevocably into the gutter.

"Terrible," the women lamented. They clutched the emaciated parcels and lumbered away as quickly as they could. At the far ends of the Avenue, in the slums of Roxbury and amid the duplexes of Mattapan, you could hear the echo.

CHAPTER II

Combined Charities

"**D**REIZEN, MY friend," the Cantor from Havana cried, turning back to his companion and clapping him lightly on the shoulder. "I am telling you what? . . . You are *in* soft with Insoft," and he chuckled at his favorite joke, belching softly. "You are going to the G&G maybe," the Cantor added casually. The Moyhel nodded his head in the affirmative. "You could lend me a dime for a cup of coffee?"

Dreizen said nothing. He reached in the threadbare pocket of a frayed and ancient tuxedo jacket. He felt with his finger through the hole of the pocket to the bottom of the coat's lining. After a moment's fumbling, a single dime rolled against the nail of his forefinger. He thrust a thumb down to catch it and bring it up. Now the thin shaving of silver shone above his eyes in the bright sunlight. He held it up as a mute testimonial of his condition.

"Didn't come . . . the check?" Insoft whispered.

"The check it didn't come," Dreizen replied, blinking back the bright sunlight and the tears with his weak eyes.

The old men stood there, frozen in their progress toward the G&G. Force of habit . . . their hands wandered down to the pockets of their trousers. They rustled the empty linings of canvas. Good strong canvas pockets in their gabardine trousers . . . the boys in the Garment District made them to last. These trousers had known better days. They longed for the former clink of fat rolls of silver. They could almost feel the dimes, quarters, and half-dollars rolling into the heap at the bottom . . . *clink* . . . *clink* . . .

Ah what a sound . . . *clink* . . . *clink* . . . *clink*.

Chink . . . Chink . . . Chink.

Dreizen and Insoft started out of their fantasies. Did they indeed hear the sound of clinking coins? Desperately their fingers trembled in their pockets.

Chink . . . Chink . . . Chink.

No, the coins were not there. And yet they could hear them clinking, rattling, or chinking. Were they going mad?

Chink . . . Chink . . . Chink.

Was it in their heads, the sound? No, it was behind them.

Chink . . . Chink . . . Chink.

They wheeled to behold, coming down Blue Hill Avenue toward them, the shadow of Tschernikoff the Mshulach. An enormous black felt coat, lined with fox skins and trimmed with a thick otter collar, flapped behind him in the warm breeze of May. Before him he bore the blue and white box of charity for the yeshivah in Jerusalem. It shook up and down with the solid rhythm of his gait, a rhythm as regular and sharp as the plea of a blind man's stick.

Chink . . . Chink . . . Chink.

The hearts of Dreizen and Insoft jumped. And

their fright was understandable. For the sight of the
Mshulach come upon you unawares was unnerving. His
left eyelid quivered up and down over his bad eye like
a nervous hummingbird. And his right eye glittered at
you from the bloodshot bars of its corners, a caged
vulture. Was he eighty . . . ninety . . . a hundred years
old? Nobody would venture to guess at the Mshulach's
antiquity. Somewhere far out on the Steppe of Galicia
he must have first appeared, shaking his little blue and
white box for Tsedokoh . . . sometime perhaps before
the first Tsars sat on the thrones of Russia and the
Tartars found the paths from Mongolia.

Over the faded black serge of his kapote, the ancient
coat of the Mshulach, hung a ragged beard in strands
of yellow and jaundiced white. It was wet with beads
of his spittle. The long formal coat, the kapote, had one
of its two buttons in back missing, and its armpits were
torn. But it exuded the invaluable smell of holiness. It
was complemented by the strammel that perched on
Tschernikoff's head. The fur strammel with its puff of
black velvet on the crown was not a cap but a relic. It
lent to the fierce demeanor of the Mshulach's face, his
shrunken cheeks and jutting jaw, the aspect of a Tartar
Prince. At first glance Tschernikoff was no other than
the great Khan Atatürk of the Golden Hordes. At second glance you might still wonder.

And yet the left-handed Moyhel and the Cantor from
Havana did not start entirely in fear. For the *chink* of
the Mshulach's blue box full of thick silver coins was
not devoid of certain musical connotations. But the task
of separating Tschernikoff from his coin was a labor for

the nimble fingers of Satan himself. Dreizen looked at
Insoft and Insoft looked at Dreizen. Usually they did
not speak to mshulachiym. A mshulach was in the eyes
of the upper clergy little better than a beggar. But in
times of trouble, Jews draw together. Perhaps they
should open up the possibility of social amenities with
their brother the Mshulach. The sense of the crisis in
Jewish affairs was uppermost in their minds. They
looked at the Mshulach and thought of Jewish fraternity. Dreizen looked at Insoft; Insoft at Dreizen. *Let
Love Prevail.* They smiled at Tschernikoff.

Tschernikoff spat on the pavement. When a Cantor
and a Moyhel smile at a Mshulach, a herring is stinking
somewhere.

"Good morning, Mr. Tschernikoff. I hope you are
having a good day?" Dreizen began pleasantly.

"Tsedokoh M'Eretz Yisroel?" the Mshulach cried,
halfheartedly holding out the blue and white box. He
knew it, the custom of centuries, Cantors and Moyhels
were not contributors.

"Ah, Mr. Tschernikoff, if only we could. As well as
you, if only we should do." Insoft shook his head
sadly.

The lines and wrinkles of Tschernikoff's brow
twisted. His eyes bulged forward slightly. In a fit of
coughing, a question rose to his lips: "Ehhhhhehhhe-
hhhehhh?"

It was an old sound. It had a patrimony of two thousand years. It was the sound of sorrow, distrust, and
suspicion. The whine of a sour wedding fiddle aggra-
vated by the heartache of the broken funeral drum. It

cannot be rendered. "You are kidding me? Am I a fool? Why do you hand me a load of . . ." All are inadequate.

"All day, Mr. Tschernikoff," continued Insoft, unperturbed, "in the cemetery I am sitting. Do I get a single El Rachamim? Wouldn't even pay for my carfare, the cemetery. As for Mr. Dreizen here, oy. A missa mshuna. A tragedy. From relief the Goyim in the post office have cut our Moyhel off. Don't have no babies, the Jews in Dorchester. In Newton, the doctors, Jews let them cut off the foreskins. Who hears of a briss anymore? In America is a terrible thing the state of our people. But from your blue and white box, I'm glad to hear, that Tsedokoh is doing *All Right.*" And Insoft attempted to pat the little container full of coins.

The Mshulach jerked his box out of reach of Insoft's fingers and deposited it in the pocket of his great coat. He wagged his head briskly to and fro, to indicate the contrary. The Tsedokoh business was in bad shape.

"Oy Mr. Tschernikoff, you can't fool me," Insoft chided him. "An A-1 Mshulach like you? That represents the finest yeshivah in Yerushalayim? On a commission basis. Soon you going to be living on Brookline Avenue."

The Mshulach stopped his brisk negative epilepsy. He looked up at Dreizen and Insoft. Then he shook his head but once, and very slowly. No . . . he would not soon be living on Brookline Avenue. The commission Tsedokoh business was not what it used to be. One time he could count on at least fifty dollars a day. Now he was lucky to bring home four or five. All morning long

he was climbing stairs. Every second door was a
Shvartza family. Shvartzas do not support Msulachiym.
And from the Jews what did he have to show? Three
dollars in change. In all of Dorchester he could count
on the finger of one hand the number of those who
would give him once a year a finiff . . . he would pause
on third-floor landings, winded and wheezing; the five-
dollar contributions crackled and danced before his
eyes.

Once, oy, once he dreamed of saving enough to go
visit that yeshivah in Jerusalem. He would wander
down the streets in the shade of palms, conversing with
the students for whom he collected. The president
would greet him. The teachers would applaud him.
Tschernikoff the Mshulach, they would introduce him
as . . . their American benefactor, a philanthropist who
had made possible the continuance of the great and
ancient yeshivah Bnai Bruk in Jerusalem.

The minarets of the great yeshivah, its mighty tow-
ers, tilted pavilions, and impregnable sun-baked walls,
crumbled in the dreams of the Mshulach. He awoke,
the dust of Blue Hill Avenue in his face; he stood on
the concrete sidewalk, between Harvard and Mclellan
streets.

What kind of community was this? What kind of
Jews, that forgot the first duty of their charity—the
support of poor sudents in l'Eretz Yisroel; the support
of their agent, the Mshulach? Didn't he represent the
most exclusive yeshivah in Jerusalem? At one time it
was considered an honor to be called on by an agent of
Bnai Bruk.

Now the Jews didn't even know what a yeshivah was. He had been forced to extreme measures. It was a question of sustenance now, not philanthropy. The Yeshivah Bnai Bruk must fend for itself. A Mshulach reduced to sleeping on synagogue benches. A shandeh!

And it wasn't as if he, Tschernikoff, hadn't taxed his own ingenuity to the fullest. Hadn't he journeyed to New York City to demand of the American National Committee of Bnai Bruk a salary? (They laughed. . . .) Hadn't he printed his own coupon books and pocketed the collections, contributions, and commission together? What more could a Mshulach do . . . short of bringing a gun along on the collections? He was thinking of switching to Community Chest. Nu, he would stick a red feather in his strammel. Would it help?

Dreizen and Insoft stared at the Mshulach. The traditional aggressiveness of his stance was no longer. Tschernikoff's shoulders hunched and sagged. His jaw was slack, his head bowed, and over the white hairs his strammel had slipped to the side, revealing a large moth hole. It was clear that here was a fellow victim of the state of Jewish affairs. The proud agent of Bnai Bruk had been reduced. Dreizen and Insoft stared at the Mshulach and his distress touched their hearts. His nakedness was uncovered. His shame was revealed. "Instead of a girdle, rags." No spoils could be shaken from such garments. For a moment they forgot their own misfortunes and sighed forth for Tschernikoff. "A Terrible Thing" formed itself silently upon their lips as they slowly shook their heads.

"A terrible thing," they lamented.

The Mshulach looked up from his spittle on the pavement. A Cantor and a Moyhel moaning forth for the fate of a Mshulach? He could not believe it. His bad eye stopped fluttering and opened wide to scrutinize them.

Nu. It was true. There were tears dripping down their cheeks. A man does not counterfeit such sentiments.

There is a saying in the Proverbs that the Almighty One, blessed be He, has, in the interests of their profession, hardened the hearts of the Mshulachiym. As they wander from land to land under the broiling sun, seeking the doorsteps of their fellow Jews, searching for the beacon of the mezuzah on the doorpost, their sympathies have been toughened and tanned to the consistency of leather. To the distress of others the Mshulach's ear is deaf. Single-minded, he pursues the gathering in of charity for his own cause.

But in every ointment there is a fly, in every seam a thread sticks out, in every man a flaw. When Tschernikoff beheld Insoft the Cantor from Havana and Dreizen the left-handed Moyhel—that they wept for his lot—his heart constricted.

And as the leather tendons of his auricles and ventricles slackened, relaxed . . . a marvel occurred. The Mshulach himself shed a tear. For the first time he felt not for himself, not for the students of the Bnai Bruk, but for his fellow Jews. In no time the heart of Tschernikoff the Mshulach was as a wet chamois. He looked about him. He looked before him. A Cantor and a Moyhel of Israel were without means. And from the tattered pocket of his greatcoat, he drew forth, with a trembling hand, the blue and white box of Tsedokoh.

Insoft and Dreizen looked at the little box of the Bnai Bruk yeshivah outstretched before them. The suppliant's paint was chipped and faded. The box's sides were pocked and battered. It looked itself like a victim. Could they refuse?

The thin shaving of silver glittered in the sun for a moment above Dreizen's head, and then he had dropped it in the box.

Tschernikoff shook the box violently in a negative direction. *No . . . No . . .* they had misunderstood. He wagged his ancient and jaundiced locks back and forth till his strammel almost fell off. He didn't want their dime. He was offering them Tsedokoh from the box. Didn't they understand?

!!!

Too late they understood. What to do? They had mistook his meaning. Tschernikoff looked at them and repeated his question by tilting the Tsedokoh box to the side. He rattled the coins inside.

Dreizen looked at Insoft and Insoft at Dreizen, then both looked at the Mshulach. He smiled sweetly at them through the stumps of his broken teeth. Wouldn't they accept his charity?

The Cantor and the Moyhel regarded the blue and white box of Tsedokoh. Was it permissible to intercept funds collected for the yeshivah students of Bnai Bruk? Times were troubled. Jerusalem was a long way off. Dorchester Jewry was in a state of present emergency. Who would miss it?

No.

No. This line of abstraction seemed dangerous. Such reasoning was not kosher. Cantors and Moyhels are not Robin Hoods.

They regarded the containerful of coins again. Was it permissible for them to accept money as an outright gift from the prosperous Yeshivah Bnai Bruk? They were accepting it via its trusted and responsible personal agent, Tschernikoff the Mshulach?

Nu.

Nu. Nu, such a gift had the taint of begging about it. With all due respects to the dignity of his person, Cantors and Moyhels are not Mshulachiym.

"Perhaps," Dreizen began in a tone that indicated nothing but the pleasure of a disinterested inquiry, "perhaps it is permissible to make a loan?"

A loan. The Mshulach, the Cantor and the Moyhel smiled delightedly at each other. A loan is a thing of business. A loan brings a sense of respect to all who participate. Loans are the prerogatives of gentlemen. Today you deal with the blue and white box of the Yeshivah Bnai Bruk; tomorrow you are transacting with the Rothschilds.

Tschernikoff the Mshulach tipped the Tsedokoh box very slightly on its side. Now how many of us have, in our childhood, attempted to extricate a coin from the little blue and white container for Eretz Yisroel? It was perched so temptingly on the window ledge of the kitchen. Who would see? One could try for hours to first tempt, then shove, finally shake the coins from the box. And on the day when the Messiah alights with his wings upon the world and the Earth is called forth for judgment, you would still be sitting by the window ledge in the kitchen, tempting, shoving, and shaking the container.

The Tsedokoh box was designed by a genius. Legend would have that it was perfected by the National Charities Board in conjunction with Chaim Weizmann and Harry Houdini. It was impregnable. What goes in does not come out, unless you possess the little key to the lock at the bottom, which is in the hands of the Charities Board in New York City. Without that key, the grand goniff of Russia himself cannot enter the box.

In every ointment a fly, in every seam a thread, in every . . .

The Mshulach was tipping the container very slowly upside down. The impossible trick was to manipulate the coins into the narrowing funnel of iron which extended into the box from the slot. You could bend it with neither fingernail, hairpin nor screwdriver. Tschernikoff shook the box gently until he felt the quarters touching the iron rim inside. He muttered a prayer and then suddenly snapped his wrist. Need I say more. Must I burden you with technical explanations? A Tsedokoh box was full. A Tsedokoh box lies empty.

Chink . . . Chink . . . Chink.

The coins came rolling out one by one.

Chink . . . Chink . . . Chink.

Clop . . . Clop . . . Clop.

Clop. Clop. Clop?

Who ever heard of such a sound from a Tsedokoh box? Was there a dybbuk inside? The old men leaned forward to examine . . . when they saw, coming down the Avenue, Druckman the Dreckman and his junk wagon. An ancient and superannuated horse, a reject of the Pohoste Glue Factory, pulled it. The horse was missing his hair in large patches. There was a question of whether there were not spots where his hide was gone too. Below his belly the flies that had followed the Shwartzekoff sisters up the Avenue were waging with his hereditary fleas a fierce battle for the possession of the flesh. The horse did not seem to care who won. He could hardly walk and his gait resembled an alte bobbe's stumbling for the last time through a cha-cha-cha. Behind him sat Druckman, hardly bothering to hold the reins. His leather cap was pulled down to the bags beneath his eyes and he appeared to be sleeping. But actually the old junkman had one eye open and was alert to the possibility of everything in the ash barrels on either side of the Avenue upward in value from a Juicy Fruit Gum wrapper.

"Good afternoon, Mr. Druckman," Insoft called. "God keep his face to you, the sun shine on you, grass in your field," he shouted by the horse's ear. "Peace and a blessing. How's the junk business?"

"Dreck," the Junkman answered laconically, with the aphorism of his profession. And it was not an inappropriate adjective to the contents of the wagon. A bundle of *Jewish Advocates*, a few bags of shmutties, and two piano stools sat in solitary discontent behind him. People no longer collected their junk to barter or sell. The iron they left forgotten in their cellars, and the paper and the rags they threw in garbage cans. What kind of a respectable junkman is it that will go picking through people's garbage cans? Nor was there a market for junk anymore. Everybody was buying firsthand on the installment plan.

"Tsedokoh M'Eretz Yisroel?" the Mshulach rasped at Druckman. A marvel is a marvel, but a customer is a customer. He held out his blue and white container. And rattled it. Inside, a single penny clattered like a hoarse clapper.

The Junkman flicked the reins and the horse abruptly stopped. Druckman leaned forward. The seat of his woolen pants showed as smooth and shiny as the wood underneath. Years had drawn the buttocks of Druckman into lean muscles, and worn the rough plank under him to a bench of polished ivory. He cocked a gleeful eye on the proffered box and called out, "Tschernikoff, you want a deal on the can?"

The Mshulach looked up to the heavens. Should he trade? Druckman bent unto his kinsman and whispered, "Anything in the wagon, and I'll throw in the horse."

The finger of Tschernikoff rose to his nose. With a ragged fingernail he counted the hairs of his nostril. A Mshulach on a horse. What would it do for business?

"Want a ride?" Druckman asked.

"Maybe you're going by the G&G?" Dreizen ventured.

"Come on," the Junkman urged.

"I'm thinking, how should we get on that wagon?" Insoft asked warily.

"It looks a little dangerous," Dreizen suggested.

"What's the matter?" Druckman replied, "Afraid? You can't get on? You know what's your trouble? Exercise! Someday instead of sitting on gravestones at the cemetery, my friend, Mr. Insoft, come out and lift bureaus. Your trouble is you got no muscles." And the Junkman leapt off the wagon to show that seventy years had not impaired the spring of his step. "Come on, I'll give you a lift." One by one he picked the old men up like children and set them on the back of the junk wagon.

"Are you sure that horse, no trouble wouldn't give?" Insoft asked timidly as Druckman climbed back to his own perch on the front of the wagon.

"Are you questioning my horse?" the Junkman asked indignantly. "An A-1 horse that knows his business aleph to noon sophiss." He flicked the reins, and Druckman the Dreckman's horse turned its head a second before beginning to clop down the Avenue, turned his shaggy mane back to the old men, proudly curled his lip and nodded at them through the stumps of broken teeth. The old men smiled at him. They were in the hands of a friend.

Thus it was with music and festivity, with the psaltery of a creaking axle and the timbrel of hooves, with the Tsedokoh box shaking like a tambourine and the voice of the Cantor from Havana sighing and singing in apprehension, that the wagon of Druckman the Dreckman bore three sages of Israel down Blue Hill Avenue toward the G&G.

"This horse, you sure, it's going fast, too much, heh?"

Dreizen looked at him. "Insoft, you could walk it faster."

CHAPTER III

Dust to Dust

HOWEVER FAST the wagon is going, let us pause. A great man is under our eyes. It's a mitzvah to do him honor. Observe in the tanned bony forearms with which he occasionally snaps the reins a sinew of iron. Observe his grip, knotted and tough. Seventy years! He holds on to life. A strong man.

And a scholar too! A pessimist who pronounces from his bench a single, shrewd truth—dreck.

Observe in Druckman the ruins of great fortunes. Ah, the Junkmen of the world! May they thrive and prosper. Workers of miracles! They resurrect the dead. They turn old into new. Is it any wonder that genii are entrusted to them? Rags and scraps they coin into gold and silver. Out of dung and dirt they scrape a treasure. Bright and shining, it glitters to them in the offal of the earth. And in America, where we are forever throwing what is ours away, hoping tomorrow for a shower of manna, is it any wonder that the junkmen grow rich?

Rich? A broch iz mir! The whole world knows of my cousin Isaac who slept under the railroad bridge in Quincy. Isaac Grobbletchick, a bum in the old country. And here too. The police chased him out of Boston. He and his burlap sack. Because if business was slow, my cousin would appropriate a little junk that was never intended, at least that soon, for his hands. From back-yard to backyard, over wooden fences and stone walls, from behind ash barrels and out of piles of leaves, the Irish police chased my cousin. And if they caught him? They left him with a face of bruises and a broken nose to stick in his borsht. A mess. Believe me, he was glad to take a snooze at night on the grass under the railroad bridge in Quincy. And in winter, when the snow drifted under too? Well, there are compensations in the life of a junkman. My cousin Isaac climbed into his burlap bag for sleep.

So what happened to Isaac Grobbletchick, whom the whole world remembers going from barrel to barrel up and down its streets, searching for a little junk?

He found it! My cousin (he doesn't admit to being it anymore) found junk. And junk. More junk! He found so much junk, he bought the land around the railroad bridge. And he began to get exclusive with the junk he brought out there. Not just any kind, you understand, anymore. He hired others to bring it in for him. Nu, a little too rusty, take it back. Too chipped and battered for my purposes, another day, thank you. A Connois-seur. An Expert. He began to buy junk from big people. Companies, firms, trusts. In no time he was dealing with the Government. He was buying tanks, battle-ships, shipyards.

And suddenly there came a war. Who started it? Was it to anyone's advantage? Yes! My cousin Isaac. It was a seller's market. The Government needed iron, steel, scrap. Who was holding it all? Guess.

All right, not all of it. Plenty of it though. Sitting by an old railroad bridge in Quincy, heaps of iron, stacks of steel, a harvest of scrap. My cousin's vineyard.

From Quincy they came to him. From Boston. From Washington. My cousin Isaac is a courteous fellow. He smiled. He rubbed his broken nose. It was in the bag. He rode through Quincy in a white Cadillac limousine, their courtesy (he had an old Jeep), a magnate, a war hero. They gave him a motorcycle escort every time he came in to have a cup of coffee, while he sat in the car and rubbed his nose, thinking, "Junk."

That was only one of Druckman's compatriots. How about Chaim Pitzell? Oh Pitzell! Pitzell! Chelsea remembers how you went from door to door begging for broken chairs. Your throat went sore from shouting in the face of slammed doors. To get rid of you, they threw them out the window at you.

You and your wife used to sit all night gluing seats to backs, backs to legs, selling them to synagogues for pennies. Chairs! Chairs! Well, how many can you handle without noticing a difference. You begin to appreciate one chair from another. Some chairs are not just to plop into. Too delicate. Too fancy. They break more easily. You can't sell a chair like that to a poor synagogue. They know better. In a minute it would break under the weight of an elder member. Three hundred pounds come down. Plotz! And it's over. Its time is up. No more chair. Take it somewhere else, Chaim Pitzell. We can't use it. Throw it away.

A man who has things thrown at him, doesn't throw things away lightly. Chaim Pitzell took the spindly old chairs elsewhere.

Eyebrows lifted. He saw the eyebrows. He lifted his own on the first offer. And turned to go. Listening for the second. On the third he turned around again. And on the fifth he shook hands, said he'd be back tomorrow and promptly went next door to the next shop to demand twice the price.

Money teaches fast. Faster than generations of culture and appreciation. Chaim Pitzell gobbled up the history of furniture with the thirst of an elephant. An elephant who has just thundered out of the desert.

An expert on antiques? Chaim Pitzell was a Professor of them. In no time, he could tell you the year, the country and the specific craftsman of every stick of furniture turned out in Europe or the Americas before the year 1900. And he was beginning to gather information about the Orient. From where? No one knew.

Except that at times during the day, an old man in a pair of gabardine pants, rotted through in the seat from sitting, was seen gliding through the public reading room at Copley Square library, tall, dusty volumes under his arms.

It wasn't in the libraries that Chaim Pitzell, however, perfected his knowledge, took his degree. He tramped up and down the dirt roads of Connecticut, Massachusetts, Maine and Rhode Island, poking in attics, rummaging in basements, crawling into sheds and boarded-up outhouses.

To make a long story short, where do you think

Chaim Pitzell found himself sitting? On a throne? I don't want to exaggerate. In America we don't sit in such high places. It's not seemly. Instead we sit at the heads of companies, corporations. We sit in plastic chairs. Even when they cost a few hundred apiece, they are mass-produced. An individual chair, made by a craftsman, is a rare thing. And who was sitting on most of them in his house in Chelsea? Why be tedious? And actually, Chaim Pitzell didn't sit in them too often. He sold them off, one by one, as slowly as he could, to people like himself, who also didn't sit too often on them.

Pretty soon, Chaim Pitzell was sitting pretty. He sat in a house not in Chelsea but on Beacon Hill, at the head of a table that shone with an old silver service and an antique satin cloth, lit by a priceless chandelier. Ah, you should sit at that table someday. His voice is so soft. Not a trace of hoarseness in it. And Mrs. Pitzell, her delicate, pink, chubby fingers. You would never guess how raw and red they were once, sticking to one another with glue.

The door never slams. There's a butler there who is instructed to be extra polite to everybody and especially to. . . . But there's nothing in the house to throw away.

You can see that our friend Druckman was not among nobodies. Yet one Junkman remains unspoken for. One, next to whom the achievements of Grobblet-chick and Pitzell are . . .

It is now for us to speak of Simon Maimon.

A stick, a bone, that's what they say he looked like.
Simon Maimon arrived alone in America, a pauper. A
rag that went by the name of a shirt, or pants, or a coat,
something, hid his nakedness. Not that it was well con-
cealed. You could see his arms, what there were of
them, his legs, his stomach and a good part of his backside. He stood on the dock and breathed air that was
his. And he was lucky to breathe it, believe me. Because he was a stowaway, and the subject of an earnest
debate between a captain from Hamburg and an agent
of the shipping line as to whether he should be thrown
overboard, dumped into the sea—well, in the case of
this skinny bit of nothing, it almost seemed humane. He
suffered within the space of a two-week passage every
disease known to man. This bundle of chicken legs that
they discovered coughing behind a wooden crate the
day after they left port. He coughed, he rasped, he spit
blood. The crew looked on and marveled. When, finally, is he going to let go of that little bit of black and
blue breath inside him?

Ah, Simon Maimon! Even then you were a miser. You
pinched back that gasp of life. You wouldn't let it go.
There wasn't enough fat on you to fry an onion in.
Above your head, you heard them. The words you
didn't understand, but a growl like that means, get rid
of him, in any language. Any decent fellow would have
jumped into the sea and saved them the trouble, for the
sake of his pride. Simon Maimon only lay, stifling the
screams that came up without his asking, making his
body jerk like a decapitated hen. His gray eyes shone in
bloodshot circles. Eh! They kicked him into a corner

and forgot about him. Where did he get sustenance?
Did he eat mice? Did he suck the ship's cat for milk?
Other men on the ship, big Norwegians with arms as
thick as a barrel, sickened, died, were tossed over.
Irishmen as stout as cattle went bad like frostbitten
potatoes and had to be dumped into the sea. Wiry
Turks turned soft as rotten plums and were cast away.
Even the English aboard began to stink in their beef
and were sent sliding into the waves. A plague rode the
ship as it tossed and turned crossing the Atlantic. And
in a broken box on the deck, a bag of bones whimpered
and gasped. Simon Maimon!

A death ship! It was quarantined for three weeks in
New York harbor. Not more than a dozen walked off
the gangplank. And no one had the energy to question
Simon Maimon's right to walk off too. I don't know.
Maybe he had someone's papers in one of the holes of
that rag.

What I know is that a no one from nowhere that no
one knew in no time became a someone. Simon Maimon
possessed a talent. He, who wouldn't swap his breath
with Death for a little peace, he, it turns out, was a
natural swapper. A trader.

What was his first transaction? All he had was that
rag. And no one would take that in exchange for anything. You wouldn't be able to give it away, with the
smell soaked into it. In fact, I wouldn't be surprised if
they had burned it on him, before he left the deck, for
the sake of the health of New York.

What did they say in Europe? The streets of America
are paved with gold. Now it's true that many, of blessed

memory, arrived but never found those streets. However, those who didn't disdain what they found under their nose in the streets they first encountered found a thing or two of value. Just on your way from the docks, in a block or two, with a quick eye, you could pick up a few nails, a horseshoe, a half-eaten apple, a broken watch. The beginnings of a business were there if you had the imagination.

Simon Maimon had plenty of that. An apple! Isn't that the fruit that God, in his sweetness, gave to our ancestors, Adam and Eve? A bitter fruit it proved, but it still sustains us. A good thing too for one prone to sickness.

And nails! Nails hold together our houses, our booths in the wilderness of America. As for a watch—what man of business is without one? Even a broken one. Time is our curse and our blessing.

In the streets of New York, Philadelphia, Chicago, Boston, Simon Maimon found nourishment. He collected, he traded, he sold and he sold. What no one wanted, he wanted. He would go anywhere to get something for nothing.

That horseshoe, what did he do with it? Throw it over his shoulder for luck? (A goyisheh kopp.) No such thing. He clapped it on the hoof of his horse.

Something for nothing! He and his wagon were off after it, no matter what.

Junk he picked up. Any kind of junk imaginable. Garbage. He actually would pick up your garbage. Of course in certain places like pig sties, garbage is valuable. A filthy business, but not for Simon Maimon. And other stuff goes begging too. Shavings, sawdust, dirt, sand, stones. Simon Maimon loaded them in his wagon and took them off where they could be appreciated. It's amazing what industry can create. Of course sometimes you have to wait awhile for a trade. You have to have someplace to dump your junk.

So Simon Maimon bought. For the first time he bought. A few acres of cheap land. Miserable land, wet, swampy marsh that bred mosquitoes and fevers. And right smack in the direction that our city of Boston was developing in.

Almost for nothing! Junk land. Every city had it. Not just Boston. Chicago, New York, Philadelphia. Who would ever think of building there? As long as they could they built elsewhere. Nasty acres with a bad odor. They built all around them. In all directions. Right around them they went. And so, in ten years, Simon Maimon found himself and his acres in the middle of Boston, New York, Chicago and Philadelphia. Suddenly people woke up! He was holding the most valuable land in town. A junkman!

A millionaire? Please. A multimillionaire.

He wouldn't sell. He leased. A piece here. A piece there. Some for ten years. Some for twenty. And he told them what to build.

A short man, Simon Maimon liked tall buildings. Into those damp acres they had to sink piles to hold them up. So what. Was he paying for them?

Of course when one Jew makes money, another hears of it. Simon Maimon became a person of note in our community. A man of wealth! You know how one is loved among us. A sign that God remembers us in our exile! He was elected to the board of first this synagogue, then that one. He sat on those pious boards too. Why not? Something for nothing. He never contributed a penny to any of them. Such was his reputation, however, that the community was grateful just for his presence. It reassured them and in fact encouraged the poorer members to give more, in the hope that Maimon might gain respect for the schul, seeing their own effort, and kick in a few dollars himself. Oh, Narishkeit!

Simon Maimon had settled here. He had taken a wife from among us. Was it for her sake that he pitched his tent among the Jews of Boston? Perhaps he liked being close to the Yankees who love to swap. And the Irish. Are they not famous for throwing things away? Empty bottles litter the streets of South Boston.

Let us go back to 1910. Maimon was not yet a millionaire. The cities were creeping slowly toward his junkyards but had not reached them. Still, he had picked up a few odds and ends here and there. Enough so that the Jews of Boston knew, bursting through the shiny blue serge suit with black grease spots on the vest, pushing against the cuffs frayed into a fringe of loose threads, sweating under the dirty blue shirt and torn woolen cap of a junkman, belted in by a worn, cracking leather strap, there was the girth of wealth.

Simon Maimon! The name was enough to frighten half a dozen Rabbis whose board of directors he sat on. Why? A little man.

Simon Maimon stood no higher than four feet five inches. He had not grown by so much as a hair since he

stumbled on legs like a chicken's down the gangplank
to America. He had expanded however. He weighed
over two hundred fifty pounds. A tiny man, his gray
eyes were barred with little red lines across the chalky
pupils. His thick fingers scratched at the stubble on his
chin. He must have used a razor he had found in the
trash with a ragged edge that scraped over his face,
leaving plenty behind. An evil, dirty appearance, the
odor of death clung to him. You were glad to give him
something to get him out of your yard or office.

He made the Rabbis uneasy, sitting, smelling of dust
in their synagogues. And yet, he had money; we knew
it; and that was a sweet enough savor in the nose of the
congregations. It was a brook of oil that washed his
feet. We rejoiced because his wealth was great. An
ornament to us, a crown upon our Torah. Ah, the fine
gold!

In the yeshivahs of Lithuania they had heard of our
pavements of gold. Here we meet one Chaim
Druckman, the son of scholars, the grandson of scholars. Poor men but each a maskil. The Talmud was in-
scribed on their foreheads, bound around their arms.
The Law was with them when they rose up and when
they sat down. It was on their tongue at the table and
in the marketplace. Even in sleep they dreamed among
the stories of the Torah.

No wonder the Druckmans sent their son to
yeshivah. His bright blue eyes shone like sunny ice at
the end of the long hall. Chaim Druckman could soon
outquote his teachers. He had a memory four thousand
years old and tripped through the commentaries of

Mishnah and Gemorah with the ease with which you rattle off the alphabet. Talmud Bavli, Talmud Yerushalemi, he leapt from one to another like a hind.

Still, what did such learning bring in Lithuania? A smile. A pinch on the cheek. A good seat in the synagogue. There were too many like him. A thousand, ten thousand, graduated each year.

But in America? Where the Jews were not in the synagogues but busy out in the streets, picking up gold bricks, stacking them in cellars and sheds; in America a *Talmid Chochem* was a rare thing.

Chaim Druckman saw his fortune. He scraped together a ruble or two from his parents, friends, teachers, and took passage. If learning had prospered in Babylon, it could do so in America.

So Chaim Druckman arrived too, on the docks of New York. He had a suit on his back and one in his trunk. A handful of letters to the learned of America. One took him to another and he was sent on to Boston. A scholar, in those days, was always treated among us with attention and respect. A fine boy, twenty-four years old, Chaim Druckman was made much of. We took him right in. My aunt Sonia gave him a room with a bed in it, a lamp, a desk—and made sure he swallowed two hot meals a day.

A Talmid Chochem! They made way for him in the synagogue, gave him a dozen honors, asked his opinion on this and that. Still, you can't go on that way forever over here. You have to make a decision. Are you a Rabbi, a businessman or an artisan? In America you have to have a profession. No loafing in the House of Study. No loitering. Not even in the presence of God.

An artisan? Chaim Druckman looked at his smooth hands. A Rabbi? Well . . . outside the schul windows, he could see the pavements glitter. And Chaim looked about the synagogue for a father-in-law to adopt him into the world of the streets. A smart boy, his bright eye had not wandered but a few feet when it lit, several pews away, on the corpulent bulk, half asleep, of Simon Maimon.

"Who's that? Oh . . . On the board? Yes? He has a daughter? Not married? Nu?"

Nu? A rumor fled up into the women's gallery. From behind a thick prayer book peered a pasty face. The daughter of Simon Maimon was no beauty. She looked down with greedy gray pupils on Chaim Druckman. Chaim didn't look up. His glance was fixed on the rise and fall of a solemn expanse. Huge and imperial, the stomach of Simon Maimon, whose unscrubbed hands were folded on this globe. The junkman snored. The whole synagogue was watching him. He blinked. And in that blink he saw Chaim Druckman out of one eye. He saw his wife and daughter in the other, put two and two together, and went to sleep on it.

At Aunt Sonia's, for the next few nights, Chaim Druckman lay sleepless. What was he getting in for? A ballagolah for a father-in-law? By all accounts Maimon was wealthy but in what? He scraped the pavements all right but not of gold and silver. His hands were filled with filth and rubbish. And he was an ignoramus who didn't understand three words of Hebrew. Maybe he was good for four or five swears in the blessed tongue, and you made an end of his proficiency. Oh, wait, the dialogue between a man and his ass. Maimon could probably footnote it.

So Chaim Druckman tried to joke with himself about the shortcomings of Simon Maimon. After all, the masters caution a scholar not to be proud. At Yavne they prayed not to feel superior to the laborer in the field. Chaim bethought himself of a hundred such admonitions and quoted himself into peace.

Then came the face of Dinah Maimon! He had caught a peek of it as he piously left the synagogue, raising his eyes for just a moment to the galleries. Someone had pointed her out among the sea of women; the gallery full of girls and ladies gossiping, mumbling, leafing through prayer books, arguing, quarreling; comparing dresses, recipes, scandals; arranging matches, divorces, separations; planning births; hoping for deaths—a regular marketplace of information with the din of a Bagdad bazaar. If down below they were praying to God, up above they were conspiring with Satan. What schemes were cooked up in that bubbling vat, the women's gallery in a Litvak schul! Who can go into them? We on the ground floor are innocent of it, and let us remain so.

Now, among the throng, a friendly finger pointed Druckman to the face of Dinah. You could not miss it. A blotchy moon stared at him with a silly, frightened look. The love of a sickly calf beckoned. For a moment his stomach filled with sour milk. He paused in the open door of the synagogue. Outside, the cobblestones gleamed with sunlight. He thought of Simon Maimon. A golden calf! He turned his face back to the gallery for a moment, though blind from the sun, and smiled.

What a wedding! I wish I could say it. Not much of a feast. Of Maimon we all expected more. A fatted calf at least should have been killed. A few chickens were done in, a few guests invited, a bottle of dry Malaga wine or two that tasted like grape juice set on the table. Not the wedding banquet that a great man gives his daughter. Chaim was disappointed, but he didn't show it to his friends. No. He tried to pour wine into mine and Aunt Sonia's cup as if the supply were inexhaustible. I saw him pour his own glass into hers when she wasn't looking.

He had married into the family of a miser. Well, he would see. A ballagolah and his horse are no match for a Talmid Chochem.

Maimon sat at the wedding table, his head just barely above it, though they had put three cushions, one on top of the other, in his chair. He poked his finger into the hole of his threadbare yarmulke, rubbing at the roots of a few wisps of smoky gray hair. He was eyeing his son-in-law. He pushed away the herring that had been set before him, his customary dish, and leaned toward Chaim, whispering sharply in a hoarse voice with the abrupt gruffness with which you drive a horse between the shafts, "Tomorrow, Boitchik! We'll talk business."

So Chaim sat down with his father-in-law at the office. An office? A shack? It was an enormous packing case with a piece of tin tacked on for a roof. The structure sagged in the middle of the junkyard whose bleak acres bordered downtown Boston.

Chaim had stayed the night in a leaky bedroom of Simon's house in the West End. A night he didn't want to remember. In the morning he and his father-in-law hitched up horse and wagon in the stable on the bottom floor and rode to work. They wound through acres of rusting bed springs, rotting mattresses, on a path just wide enough for the wagon. "My inheritance," thought Chaim. Beds where seed had gone bad and age had shivered its last. Stained with the blood of dead hopes and illusions. He looked across the melancholy fields, a valley of iron bones: bureaus, desks, chairs—broken limbs—and at the farthest corner, garbage dumped there to decompose that stank across Boston. Manure! Something would grow here. He would cultivate it. The morning sun streaked through the junkyard, gilding it with rosy hues.

In the shack, Simon faced his son-in-law, seated on a barrel across a lopsided table.

"Nu?" asked Chaim.

A little smile crept onto the Junkman's face. "You want a wagon?"

Chaim looked at the gray stubble of his father-in-law's face. An ugly customer.

"Ballagoltchick," he answered sarcastically, "you got books?"

"Books, mine pisher?" asked Simon. He looked around the office of his packing crate. An old stove pushed its blackened stack through the tin roof; an oak table tilted to the side; two broken barrels sat stolidly on the earth floor—these were the only fixings or records of the existence of Maimon & Co.

"Books!" he echoed and thrust a thick hairy arm into the inner pocket of his grease-lined suit. Two little green pamphlets were drawn forth, pinched between his fingers. He put them down on the table. Opening first one, then the other.

The book on his left hand had a row of figures in it. The last one recorded read $200,000.00. The book on the right read $50,000.09.

Chaim looked the Junkman in his gray-crimson eyes. He spit to the side. "With books, mine Ballagoltchick, it'll double."

Simon scratched his fingers on the splinters of oak. He spit to the other side. "Nu?"

So his father-in-law bought Chaim a set of books. He didn't buy them exactly. He picked them up somewhere. The leather was peeling off their backs and the name of their old firm was almost legible on the frayed cloth covers. A few pages were covered with scribbles and figures, but they were easily plucked out and the firm of Maimon & Co. made to rule exclusively within their neat ordered blue lines.

Up and down the columns flew the figures of Chaim Druckman as he inventoried—digging and scraping out of his father-in-law's memory what was on his acres in Boston, Chicago, New York and Philadelphia.

As the price of scrap copper or tin went up in one place and down in another, Chaim's mind leapt from yard to yard, comparing prices. It skipped as easily and

as shrewdly as it had from Mishnah to Gemorah, from
Bavli to Yerushalmi. Sell here! Sell there! Chaim
showered a series of orders on the thick head of his
father-in-law and the figures in the green bankbooks
bore him out. Simon did all the buying or picking up.
Chaim didn't even want to know where the stuff came
from. He only cared who wanted it and got rid of it as
high as he could.

It was a great age for junkyards. In Europe, nations
were turning each other into just that. World War I!
The price of iron, steel, tin, paper—shot up. You know
what Grobbletchick made out of the mess. Simon
Maimon had not been able to find any battleships for
nothing or be assured he would have loaded them into
his wagon and taken them off. He had found enough,
however, with Chaim finding places to sell at the highest premium, so that the two banks on State Street
where he dumped his cash began to send a Vice President to hold the door open for the fat little man in a
baggy, patched suit who left his horse and wagon by
the curb outside. And in the street, they tipped their
bowlers to his ragged woolen cap.

The problem was to get enough junk! Wait! We'll go
into this in a moment.

What was Chaim's relationship in this business? He
was the brains. Maimon was the brawn. And Maimon
made sure that Chaim was muscled out of the cashbox.
They began to fight. "What am I getting out of it?"
shouted Chaim. "Bubke! Chicken feed! What's going
on?"

"You get a salary."

"Pennies. Shticklach! I'm making thousands for you every day."

"It's in the family."

"Let it be in my pocket."

Back and forth they quarreled. Chaim swore at his father-in-law in English, Yiddish, Russian, Polish, German and Hebrew. In a vicious mood he even threw in a little Aramaic. Maimon gave him a house in Dorchester, just to get Chaim away from his ear at night. He was not at home in the world of words.

And Chaim Druckman in those days had a mouth that could curse and quote. No one had put a hot coal in his mouth as was done to Moses. Right and left, he abused his father-in-law. "Ballagolah! You know what God threatens Israel with? I'll make your heavens iron and your earth brass. Leviticus! That's you. Only you received an additional share. A brain of brass too! You think you pick up a son-in-law for nothing? Am I an ass? Do I get a share of oats? You live like a pig in the garbage. My father-in-law, the king of the Chazars. I'm married to royalty. Last of the big-time shnorrers!"

Not just in the home among the family, before Simon's wife and daughter, did this go on. In the schul too. If someone there, trying to be respectful, asked Maimon a question, his son-in-law butted in. "What does *he* know? An expert on dreck! You want an opinion on that, he'll give it."

The congregation was uncomfortable in the face of this abuse. Maimon's wealthy acquaintances shifted uneasily in their seats.

Simon said nothing. He smiled in the face of it. He

saw the figures climbing in the bankbooks. What could
his son-in-law do? A hasty tongue, let him rattle on.
Simon shook hands in the synagogue as if he heard
nothing behind his back. The insults fell on an ear of
cast iron.

Chaim saw quickly that the blows of his tongue were
becoming nothing to his father-in-law. Feathers that
tickled his vanity. The more he abused, the more Simon
was amused.

It didn't bring honor on him to curse Simon in front
of the whole Synagogue. It didn't bring him anything
else either. Chaim conceived of a new strategem. A
partnership! Let the old man make him a partner in the
business, give him a share.

For this, Chaim turned to his wife.

Poor Dinah, one of those girls who is locked in the
house as a child and grows up pale as a flounder. Her
father regarded her as something strange. A bargain he
acquired for what he ordinarily pished away. Like her
mother, he found a few rooms in his tumbling house
and stored her there for some future use. And the
Maimon women stayed there, seldom seeing sunlight
except on the Sabbath. Then they floundered like fish
from some dark channel of the sea into the women's
gallery, in ill-fitting dresses. The wealthy Maimons
were the objects of bewildered respect, confused laughter; gossip lapped about their seats but seldom touched
them.

And who should swim into the bed of the colorless
Dinah? A swordfish, Chaim Druckman. If the wedding
night was a bad dream to him, to Dinah it was a night-

mare of delight. Who knew that such things were possible? Not even the women's gallery and its wild talk had foretold it. She wallowed in her juices the next morning like a wounded tuna, bloody but happy.

Chaim, as you know, had gotten up as early as possible and left for the junkyard. When he came home she turned to him with such love—her breasts ached. She followed him around the house, listing from side to side, as if on flippers. All day she waited for the night and she fell on him in the bed like a whale. What could Chaim do? He surrendered and flowed into the tide.

Out of bed, she was his slave, his little flotsam. Chaim could have done without it. He was grateful to get to the junkyard each morning and to go to the synagogue every night and on holidays. What a relief that the women were seated apart there.

Among the benches, he found a few friends. Old schoolfellows from the yeshivah who had decided to come themselves to the New World. He stayed up as late as he could with them, trading stories, jokes, opinions. Discussing the world and its problems. To them the son-in-law of Maimon was a mighty man, despite his outcry that he was kept on pennies. Chaim owned a new house in Dorchester. He dressed like a banker. Nu! They had just come over and were living on pennies. They knew what a penny meant.

Chaim knew what a penny meant too. He was making a pretty one for his father-in-law. So he turned back to his wife for a moment. Instead of rushing off to the synagogue after his day in the junkyard, he came home.

Chaim for supper? Dinah Druckman stumbled around the table grateful as a cow whose udders are bursting with milk. And when Chaim took her hand between his fingers. Ah!

He told her briefly. "Puppicknick! I'm making your father a millionaire. He's making me a pauper. We have to have a share in the business! Or else . . ." He pushed her away. "F'arsheteist?"

Dinah didn't f'arshetay completely. She understood a little. And that was enough. As if someone had smacked her head against a post.

She went that night to her father's house. She went to her mother's room. They came out and went to the kitchen, where Simon was sitting having a glass of tea by himself. And they started in, "A share! A share!" That's all Maimon heard for two months. He went to Chicago—they sent him postcards, "A share! A share! Give him a share! Your own son-in-law."

And Druckman threatened to quit, to make less money for him, to do this and that. It was a wonder that Maimon didn't junk the lot of them.

Instead, one day, he wheezed and said, "An eighth."

Druckman couldn't believe it. He even smiled at the old Ballagolah. After all, he was his partner. An eighth in Maimon & Co., as he knew from the books, was nothing to sniff at.

Was Chaim happy? As the days passed he found out that his eighth didn't entitle him to anything for a while. Not until Simon either pleased or dropped dead. His father-in-law paid him the same salary. He had a percentage, but he wasn't allowed to collect any of it. All the profits went into Maimon's bankbooks.

Yet Chaim had position. As the son-in-law and partner of a wealthy man, and as a scholar, our community treated him with deference. He sat on the V'aad Ha'ir—the council of the city—and watched over the Kashruth of Boston.

Chaim was one of those entrusted to make sure that milk did not mix with meat in Jewish restaurants, that cows in our city that went to the Jewish butchers had their throats cut in strict accordance with the Law. A high honor! Only in his own yard, things were not kosher. Junk was at a premium. How to get it?

Simon snatched it. He stole it. He paid Boss O'Shea for exclusive rights to all the junk of the city of Boston. A deal! For life, O'Shea got a hundred dollars a week. Maimon got junk. High-class junk it was too. Brass fittings from old streetcars, iron sewer pipes—quality scrap. The other junkmen went black in the face. They barked in public. A crook! A dog! Too late. Maimon had snapped up the bone. He hustled off to his yard with it. He had pulled a deal on the Boss. A hundred dollars a week? Hundreds of thousands in cash rolled into Maimon's bankbooks.

The hundred, of course, was paid under the table. Money was moving around outside the columns of Chaim's books. It made him nervous.

And, even when you deal under the table, you have to play your cards straight. O'Shea was thrown out. Maimon cut off the hundred dollars that was set aside for him each week. O'Shea sent a note, "The deal was for life."

Maimon sent a scrap of paper back, "You lost your cards."

Chaim protested. All right, O'Shea wasn't holding anything in his hands anymore, but a deal is a deal. A hundred dollars was a pittance. You don't kick a man when he's down. You made a fortune off him. Even among thieves there has to be honor. Maimon snorted. O'Shea was on the junk heap. He, Maimon, wasn't giving something for nothing. Let O'Shea complain to the police. Eh? They'd put him in jail.

Chaim didn't like it. The old Junkman was stealing, then cheating. It wasn't kosher.

The business was getting shady. Not just under the table. Simon knew all the crooks and no-goods in Boston. They knew how to get something for nothing. It was the twenties. Bootleg liquor—bootleg junk. Late at night, when only the cops were up, trucks, not wagons, were arriving at the junkyard, dumping newly broken statues, slightly used cars, spotless steel girders. They were buried under the old rubbish. Chaim found that he had a new kind of junk on his hands.

Strange men came to the office to see Simon. Men as short as the old man, but dark and small-boned. Slight, in polished black shoes and loud but expensively tailored suits, they pulled him into the corner and began to shout in Italian. The Junkman pretended not to understand. He pulled out a roll of bills and peeling off a few, stuffed them into their breast pockets under the inevitable white handkerchief. The little men, counting the bills, cursed. Simon stepped absentmindedly on their shoes if they shouted too loud. Ugly scenes. Someone shot a few bullets through the thin walls of the shack one afternoon. Maimon came in one morning, his broad face wrapped in a bandage. The bruises crept out from under the white gauze, blue, red, brown where the blood had dried. He smiled and mumbled, "Down the stairs." It was an accident. Except that, the day before, Chaim had seen an Irish face in the door of the office, a mug of purple anger, shaking a fist. Simon had seen it, too, and spit in its direction.

The old man dismissed the threats that Chaim heard here and there. Only looking at Simon, his face scratched and grizzled as a pig's, Chaim knew. His father-in-law wasn't kosher.

Something at home wasn't kosher either. That smack on the head. It had done something to Dinah. Her gray eyes lost their glossy light. They went dull, without luster. She no longer floundered about eagerly after him.

He had turned away from her again, after the share business was settled. He noticed she didn't cling to him so much after this. Well, so what? She didn't say anything. One night, in bed, he turned to her, restless, putting his arm around her playfully. Her eyes opened wide. She lay rigid. Her legs locked together tight as an oyster. And she stayed that way. Nu, it wasn't kosher.

Chaim wasn't sure what was wrong. Only he was drowning in the world of the Maimons. At least he had to get out of the old man's business and set up for himself.

During one of their fights over Maimon's business techniques, the Junkman had said to his son-in-law, "You want out? I'll give you a hundred thousand for the share."

Since then, in the synagogue or marketplace, whenever Chaim tried to shame, Simon would turn and ask with a shrug, "A hundred thousand?"

A hundred thousand! The stock market charged and surged. America was a crazed crowd of speculators screaming approval at its mad antics. Up and down it sprang, higher and higher, as if it would jump over the moon for them. A Talmid Chochem that has studied Babylonia Talmud knows something about the moon. Why should ignoramuses make money? If fools were growing rich, how about wise men? Chaim boasted to his friends at the synagogue who were dabbling themselves—"Let the Ballagolah give me the cash. Watch! A bull? For me, it'll spawn calves of gold. What can I do? A klotz. He has his nose in the garbage."

So now, between the shade of his father-in-law's business and the bright promise of the market, Chaim decided to take the old man up on his offer.

"A hundred thousand?" asked Simon when Chaim complained of the leaking roof in the shack.

"All right," said Chaim.

The old Junkman looked at his son-in-law. Maimon's face contracted into a dozen bottomless wrinkles. Surprised, he drew his breath slowly. He looked hard at Chaim's sparkling blue eyes and he looked past the younger man through the open door of the shack. It was raining. In the misty gray, buildings rose high and mighty. The Talmid Chochem had his back to them. He couldn't see the city, creeping right to the edge of the junkyard.

"All right," said Maimon. He leaned over the table. "You going to—what?"

"Stock."

"Pick it up for nothing?"

"Practically."

Simon laughed. It became a throaty cough, deep and hacking.

Chaim Druckman laughed to himself. An alter kaker. The old fool would soon blink.

He plunged with a hundred thousand. Into the market! His money started to go up, to climb on the margin, to skip on the mountains of stock. And then, a God, awful to behold, cut the throat of the market. With one blow, swift and terrible, He severed its artery and in a few moments it bled to death. In the flood, Chaim among many others was swept down from the mountains of hope. Dashed to his knees. Knocked off his feet. Dazed by the sudden fall, he wandered through the depths of despair. He was abashed and penniless.

Chaim Druckman walked the streets a poor man. Under him the sidewalks were spotted with vomit and poverty. His father-in-law was not even in the city to laugh at him. Boss O'Shea had come back to power and Simon thought it wise to retire to Florida. On the telephone, he managed his acres through others. They had begun to see the value of the junk land and were doing all the work of clearing for him. Cities are like children,

even in bad times they grow. People were holding on to
their junk now. It was a good time to go into real estate.
Chaim saw the buildings go up on his father-in-law's
land. And he laughed. A black laugh. He walked
through the junkyard. His father-in-law was right.
What did he know about? Junk! That's what he, Chaim,
had made of his life. He kicked a can. Twisted iron
beds, abandoned cars with birds and insects nesting in
the seats; everything rusting or going to seed. A hand
stroked his head. It was a teacher at the yeshivah pat-
ting his yarmulke, predicting a great future for the little boy. Tears of his parents blinked in his eyes as he
waved a careless good-bye, taking a last leave. Looking
toward the skyscrapers going up, he saw the golden
turrets of the palaces he had dreamed of ruling. . . . Eh!
He looked at the rusty can. Its cover showed a sharp
edge, here and there. Would it cut against his wrist?

Chaim's heart was black. What was he good for? He
tried the coal business. On a commission basis. But
things were too hot for people in those days. They
bought as little coal as possible. Chaim trudged up and
down the streets trying to sell the lumps of fuel. Too
many lumps were rattling in his heart. People didn't
buy from him. Buy from a man with a black face? They
shut the door on him, as if he were the Angel of Death.

One day, who should he meet in the street? Boss
O'Shea. It seems that the Boss had heard of Chaim's
effort on his behalf. He saw him in reduced circum-
stances, a hole in his pants, his hands coarse and dirty.
In those days it came to pass (for a while) that black
turned white. "Selling coal, Mr. Druckman?"

"Yes, yes," Chaim mumbled, wanting to break away, ashamed. The Boss took out a pad and scribbled a sentence on it. He pressed it into Chaim's hand and rejoined his cronies, who were waiting for him at the corner of the block. Chaim looked at the slip. It was an order for one hundred tons of coal. The city of Boston would pay for it to be delivered to the poor of South Boston. Ah, Chaim felt for them and himself.

Junk! With the lowly is wisdom. With the bit of profit he made from the coal sold to the city for the poor, Chaim bought a horse and wagon. Junk!

Simon Maimon died in Florida; a cancer had spread through his body and made trash of him in no time. "Junk!" cried Chaim, hearing the news. There was no inheritance. Income Tax! Maimon had thought, "Why should they get something for nothing?" After his death, the Government gobbled up his estate in taxes and fines. If they hadn't, there would have been no inheritance anyway. Maimon had left the money to his daughter's children—if she had any. A joke. Dinah lay at home, rotting in her own flesh. "Junk!" cried Druckman. He was ashamed to go to the synagogue. His friends there would remember his boasting, the insults he heaped on old Simon: "The Ballagolah, a shnorrer, fit to drive and screech, just right for a horse and wagon." "Junk!" he shouted. Dust he saw in all directions. The pavement below him was black, the streets littered with ashes, his tongue too. "Junk!" he shouted. Up and down the streets of Dorchester, with his horse and wagon, "Junk!"

CHAPTER IV

A Pleasure Ride

THE WAGON wound down the steep incline of Blue Hill Avenue from Franklin Park to Franklin Field. Although the box of the cart shook and its springs clattered, the wheels rolled smoothly over the soft asphalt carpet. Its nubble shone black and oily under the midday sun.

"A nice ride," said Dreizen.

"Cobblestones, remember?" Insoft jabbed the sky with his arthritic finger. "Trolley tracks, holes! Just walk across!" He stood up in the wagon. "Trip, fall, break your neck."

What happened? How did we come by this fine dark asphalt on Blue Hill Avenue? Our politicians never cease to brag—they got it. Fifty years it took. When the Irish Democrats grabbed hold of the city council, street repairs stopped just outside of South Boston. To get the Avenue paved, one had to connive and threaten. We would get the Commonwealth to take it over; it would be a Federal Highway; we would cede it to the State of Israel. In my window I hung a sign—"Vote Republican." Finally they repaired it. What happened?

"Where's everybody?" asked Dreizen. The sidewalks of the upper Avenue were bare.

"Where? You know!" shouted Insoft, lurching forward. "Belmont, Newton, Brookline. They fixed the Avenue. Just in time. Everyone drove away on it."

A lovely black highway right in the middle of Dorchester but too late. One good deed amid a multitude of sins. In winter, snowplows from the city never quite reached Dorchester. In summer, garbage collections were slow. The streets were left dirty and unwashed.

"If I made a little money, I'd move away too," sighed Dreizen before lapsing into silence.

Along the sides of the Avenue, every few hundred feet, an enormous old Dutch elm spread the scarred gray tissue of its limbs, almost too ancient, it seemed, to bear the birth of bright green foliage each spring. Like a row of stolid gray teeth, the elms gritted their roots upon the pavement. They maintained themselves like the storekeepers who dealt under them, in the sullen pride of a former flourishing. From between the trees reeked the breath of Blue Hill Avenue: the smell of bad herring and stale fruit, freshly butchered meat and rotting vegetables. Now and then, for some reason, an elm was missing. It showed as a gap, a missing tooth, and soured the expression of the Avenue.

The wagon was now moving faster, rolling headlong down the sharp slope of the Avenue. And the Junkman's horse in response to twin inducements—the force of gravity pulling him forward, the threat of the heavy cart behind—broke into a step that resembled, in faltering degrees, a trot.

Druckman leaned forward to encourage his horse. He called out to it in Hebrew:

He paws in the valley.
Rejoices in his strength:

The horse picked up its tattered ears.

With storm and rage
swallows the ground.

A quotation from Job? Was it applicable?

The glory of his snorting is terrible
Haa! Haa!

The horse began to make an effort. After all, it had
been Druckman's companion for years now. To it alone
he unburdened his heart. A man may have a weight
heavier than any harness. Pressing his sunburned cheek
against its shaggy flanks, a hand over its neck, he had
whispered such secrets into its ear—"Haa!" Yet a good
man. How many creatures get a real rest from Friday
night to Sunday morning? Whose masters bring them
late at night, a feast from their own table? Many a time
the Junkman slept in the stable in preference to his own
bed.

And now, in order not to shame his friend before the
old men, the horse stretched his creaking limbs.

Downward they rolled past Mclellan Street, past the
rows of houses which fronted the Avenue: three-family,
six-family, eight-family, twelve-family. They rolled past
sprawling wooden buildings, crossbreeds of mansions
and tenements. Rotting Corinthian pillars tilted toward
them. The sagging porches hardly supported the
weight of a few old ladies. No one waved to them. The
old lay outside in rocking chairs and mildewed sofas to

die in the sun. Once the empty houses had boiled with children. The young bubbled out of windows, across and off the porches, onto the lawns. In the close air of bedrooms and hallways, Israel's seeds spawned and multiplied. The Chronicler would shake his head over the number. There was a tumult in the passages that shook the long cords of the electric bulbs and battered the plaster. Shouts and screaming shattered the windows. Stairs collapsed. The smell of fish and cabbage, fresh bread and gravy, was so thick in the halls, it flowed out the open front doors like soup. And now?

Empty windows eyed the swift descent of the Junkman. Half the apartments were unrented. Inside, it was deathly still. Only the screams of the Beth Israel Ambulance disturbed the quiet. The small cough of the tubercular could be heard. The smells in the hall were dry and dusty. Watermarks on the wall remained where life had bubbled.

On churned the wagon of Druckman. On past the gasoline stations. On swept the four sages. Tattered flags and banged-up signs swung toward them in the wind. Past the meager windows of the wholesale cigar stores, past the decaying displays of the variety stores, faster and faster, the wagon rolled: the Mshulach, his greatcoat flapping; the Moyhel, his smile disappearing; the Cantor, his breath coming hard.

"Hold on to your hat," called the Junkman to Tschernikoff.

"A cold! I'm catching one!" Petrified, one hand at his throat, still standing, swaying, clutching the sparse hair of the Moyhel's head, Insoft cried, "Please, Druckman, my voice! Think of it!"

"My insurance ran out," Dreizen mumbled. His bony left hand gripped the wooden slats of the sides so tight his fingernails winced. His hair was on end.

For now they rolled downward with a furious rush past the Mayor's Public Housing Project. It loomed to the side where, perched high on a cluster of rocks above Blue Hill Avenue, a pack of Goyim and Shvartzas looked down on the rest of Dorchester. The horse galloped as if mad. Sweat broke out in beads along his flanks. A ragged tail shivered in the wind. "Stop a second! Let me get off!" shrieked Insoft. The wagon clattered, shook, trembled, vibrated. It lifted its wheels above the asphalt and skipped. The axle spun by itself. The horse did not touch the ground. Druckman was somewhere in the air. Faster and faster they fell. The end was approaching. The bottom of the incline rose under their noses. *No* glared the traffic light. A host of frightened cars hid behind it. *No* it glared in bloodshot red. *No?* Who could say *No* to the steed of Druckman the Dreckman? "Haa! Haa!" The horse pawed the air. His hooves sung with sparks. He soared.

CHAPTER V

Between Heaven
and Earth

WHAT? THE horse was where? In the air? Oh, maybe you don't believe me? You don't want to call me a liar, but there are other names.

You think I have the story flying through the air? Listen! A liar is an abomination to God. I know it! I told you the story straight out. No twisting, turning or pinching to make it act like a nudnick. I gave you the facts, nothing but.

The horse was in the air. The wagon too and all its contents. High over Dorchester.

"Too fast! Too fast!" wailed Insoft. "We went too fast!" The Moyhel's left hand beat the air like the wing of an angel. The Mshulach began to add and balance his receipts. They might land in heaven or at the Yeshivah Bnai Bruk. In either case, he was a little short. A bedraggled fur cap flew around him.

Down below, our friends could see Goyim and Shvartzas flashing knives in the alleys of the Public Housing Project. Franklin Field, a patch of dirty green, stretched to their left; to their right, tiny iron fence pales, the sharp spikes of the Mattapan Insane Asylum's twisting fence. A bad place to land! Yet they ascended. Like Elijah, who rose to the Heavens in a chariot. "My soul," Insoft whispered, arms trembling, "my soul, it's pure. Take it above . . ."

All right! I see your finger at your ear. Don't scratch. You don't have to believe me. For right here on the shelf, I got a first hand, on-the-spot, eye-witness account in an affidavit. Crack the seal and see for yourself.

CHAPTER VI

An Affidavit

Know all men by these presents that I, Max Kupperstein, of 12 Wildwood Road in the Mattapan district of Boston, County Suffolk, and Commonwealth of Massachusetts, on oath, depose and say that the following facts constitute the truth, the whole truth and nothing but the truth, so help me God.

ON WEDNESDAY, May 5, I traveled by taxicab in the company of single fare, Itzik Bibble, via Harvard Street in the direction of the Blue Hill Avenue intersection. At approximately between three and four P.M. or somewhere around that time, I picked up this fare Mr. Bibble in front of the State Hospital for the Mental in Mattapan; and gettin' out in front of the front gate of the Nut House, I assisted this Mr. Bibble in the back seat where he wants to go. Old Mr. Bibble tells me he don't want to go nowhere. So I get up from the front seat to take him out of the back seat. But then he says drive him to his daughter-in-law, Mrs. Yanover Bibble, at 46 Warner, so I get back into the front seat.

"Where would you go if you could go somewhere?"

Bibble asks me and he begins to cry. He cries like a little boy. An old man cryin', it isn't a pretty thing. I told him I'd go home and have a good nap.

Mr. Bibble don't give me no answer but sticks his thumb in his mouth and sucks. Well, what can you do? I start up my taxi and drive via Harvard Street in the direction of the Blue Hill Avenue intersection.

Now even though Mr. Bibble was sittin' back there, suckin' thumb, he can tell you that with my drivin' there was nothing wrong. I was in A-1 inspection order. So for what happened, don't blame me. In the front of my head two eyes I got—on the road like radar. And in the back of my head I got eyes too. To drive in Boston, believe me, you practically got to have eyes in your toches.

Why? Well of course we got rules for drivin'. But in Boston everyone knows the Mayor. And if not the Mayor, well a City Councilor will do. To tell the truth, you don't even need a City Councilor; the cop on the corner will call his brother and fix the ticket. So who pays attention to rules? Out-of-*townahs?* They leave their cars outside the city. They better not try.

We got other troubles, worries. Here and there, at certain times of day, on our highways and intersections we have a little snarl that our Traffic Engineers cannot make come out straight.

Be frank, though. If you're dealin' wholesale, what is Boston traffic? Compared to New York City, Chicago, Los Angeles—Boston traffic is a pish in the bucket. With *all* our dead ends, phoney intersections, streets that go nowhere; those cities and their traffic . . . we're swamped.

But perhaps you're not interested just in wholesale lots. Perhaps you would like to take a look at a little quality goods? If so, give a listen. We got in Boston a nasty driver. We got here the nastiest bastards on four wheels. Excuse me. I didn't mean to swear in the affidavit. But I'll be honest. If you can't swear, give up drivin' in Boston. You won't get out of your driveway.

I don't have to say why. Everybody in Boston knows why everyone drives so nasty! This is the city where the Yankee hates the Irish, and the Irish don't care for the Italians, and the Italians could do without the Shvartzas, and the Jews hate everybody. But the Irish hate everybody too and so does everyone else. In fact the Irish hate the Irish. But that's only been happenin' recently, since there are so many of them. So never mind. When you go out to drive, it isn't just to get somewhere, it is to pick on your neighbor a little, to see if you can't beat him across a traffic light or steal his right of way or keep him from passing you in a four-lane highway. That's it, just crowd a little to the left at twenty miles an hour, oh, oh, a little to the right now. Listen to him honk his horn. Is he mad. Ha!

There are many corners in the city where you can play tricks. However, for all the time I've been drivin', for variety you can't match our own intersection at Harvard Street, Talbot Avenue and Blue Hill.

A little history. I drove a cab in Boston when Clarkwood Street was Clark's farm and most of Dorchester, like Franklin Field, grass and dandelions. On Blue Hill Avenue I could have bought lots for nothing, for the price of a fare up and down the Avenue. People begged me—take the land off their hands. When I think of it, drivin' along, I get sick in the taxi.

Anyway, till a few years ago there was no light at the intersection of Talbot, Harvard and Blue Hill. I know because for *fohty* years I bent people's ears to get one. The worst corner in Boston. Not a single cop ever stood there.

With good reason. Down from Codman Square come a pack of Irish Goyim, all crazy. Gunnin' motors, crackin' exhaust pipes, throwin' beer cans, they rush along Talbot Avenue, yellin', swearin', toward the Blue Hill Avenue intersection. Make way! It's a drag strip! They grabbed hold of city hall. They get the right of way on every street in Boston. Didn't they paint all the traffic signs green?

To us Jews, the right-of-way on Blue Hill Avenue is a matter signed and sealed. Didn't Abraham make a covenant with God? It included Blue Hill Avenue. As long as we live here. From Grove Hall to Mattapan the Avenue is choked with Jews and their cars, wagons, trucks, pushcarts, bikes, taxis, kiddie carts. It's a sin to give up the right of way. Like forgettin' about your share in Eretz Yisroel. A thought that doesn't cross the mind of a pious Orthodox.

To stand in the middle of this, blow a whistle and bleat! King Solomon couldn't do anythin' with this corner.

On the Wednesday, May 5, that I was talkin' about when I started, I was travelin' by taxicab with my single fare, Mr. Bibble, thumb in mouth, down Harvard Street toward that corner and the light they put up there to play games with the traffic. This afternoon they even got a cop to sign away his life and stand at the intersection.

I was in a hurry. No runnin' up an extra nickel or two on the meter. I don't pay no attention to the stop sign but hit the brakes right at the edge of traffic.

So then I have to wait ten minutes. No wonder they got a cop there. Cars are jammed into each other's tailgates. Someone finagled with the light at Morton Street again? The intersection is like a bunch of millin' cows penned in between the sidewalks. Each one has a nose up his neighbor's exhaust pipe. Finally, a lady with a Willy's Jeep full of screamin' babies stops and lets me cut in. She is right behind a truck loaded with cabbages. I wedge myself under the tailgate. Now, everytime we jolt forward a foot, a cabbage hits the windshield. Beggars can't be choosers. I'm just inching out from behind the truck in front of an old Pontiac I'm sure I can fool into stallin', when the wagon appears.

A wagon in the air! A horse flyin'! Spread-eagle, and behind it a box of old men with beards, shoutin' and prayin'! In the air!

Mr. Bibble wasn't the only one with a thumb in his mouth.

I looked to the intersection. The cop has in his mouth a whole hand. He's whistlin' on five fingers. But the wagon can't be stopped. And the cop's face is turnin'

green. He puts a hand up to stop Talbot Avenue traffic.
Everything would have been all right, a few broken
bumpers, one less junk wagon and the loss of a horse.
For up and down Blue Hill Avenue, traffic began to
move fast.

But at this moment *Someone* chose to ally Daniel H.
Dropnick & Funeral Home with the Goyim of Talbot
Avenue.

Who could believe their eyes? Who wanted to? What
do we see speedin' up Talbot Avenue, approaching the
intersection at fifty miles per hour—a funeral procession. In the lead car, a Lincoln Continental hearse with
bulletproof windows and gold-plated chrome, Daniel
Dropnick himself, followed by twelve Cadillacs and a
truck full of flowers, flowers enough to put up a Garden
show, everythin' from the Governor's secretary's garde-
nias to the bunch of deadly nightshade that came from
the Boston Home for Unwed Mothers; carnations,
roses, orchids, daffodils, from all the Unions and Veteran's organizations in the City, even a large potted
palm from the Massachusetts Bar Association. This
truck, rushin' along at fifty miles per hour trying to
catch up with the rest of the procession, is shakin' like
one of the hangin' gardens of Babylon. Danny is in a
hurry. He wants to get to the crematorium with an old
friend, Lennie the Shtup. That morning Lennie is discovered in the trunk of his Volkswagen in three pieces,
parked across the street from an aunt's house in Brookline. There is enough lead in him to cast a full-size
statue for over the grave. The coroner ruled suicide.

But the FBI is interested. So Danny wants to get to the cemetery fast and melt Lennie down.

In such a hot situation you couldn't expect that Daniel Dropnick would give you the right of way. But ordinarily he wouldn't give you the right of way either. He wouldn't give you the right time, the right change. . . . Half the time he wouldn't give you the right name. That's what happens when you stick your nose into dirty business. Not that every pimp, crook and cop in Boston didn't know who he was—all three hundred pounds. Our Undertaker! One thing he would give you, a punch in the nose.

Someone dies in your house? A moment later, Danny and his boys walk in. You're prayin' over a warm body but Danny snatches it up swearin' and walks out the door. If you reproached him or, God forbid, crossed him, such threats he would shake at you. The first words out of his mouth—"Shmuck, I'll kill you. And then I'll do somethin'. They won't put you in the grave before we play some tricks. Someday I'll get hold of you. Down you'll go, one leg shorter than the other. Where will your eyeballs be, eh? I'll cut off your petzelle and chew on it. Nu! Your balls will be in your mouth. Then let your wife stand over you and pray." Such horrible things. This is our Danny!

So how did it happen this bum had power in the district? Well, how many families can afford after a long illness to bury their own? In a poor Jewish district, not many. But you know we got pride. Better to owe the undertaker than ask for charity. So half the district owes Danny somethin'. Come election time—

Danny reminds us, and points to his favorite candidate.
A good fellow, he'll even come into the votin' machine
with you and push on the levers.

And now he and his funeral procession were pushin'
down Talbot Avenue at fifty miles an hour, goin' with
the speed of a crazy man toward the Blue Hill intersection. The cop has his hand up. So what? Boston cops
are a dime a dozen. He can push them too. They all get
a free case of Manischewitz at Easter. Danny sticks his
hand out and waves. Let the cop make way for him.
Get the traffic out of his way. The cop don't wave back.
The cop just jumped into a passin' convertible. And just
at this moment, Danny reaches the edge of Blue Hill
traffic, realizes that comin' toward him fast . . .

Fast? Gevuuuuuuult . . . It was on top of him. A junk
wagon in the air? The M.T.A. bus is right in front of
him. *Smash! Crash!* He was in the air too.

Dowwwwwwwwwwwnnnnnnn he came on top of an
old Pontiac. *Smack!* A Willy's Jeep was comin' at him
from one side, children screamin', a truck full of cabbages from the other. Oooooowwwwwwwww! They
whacked him. Foxie's Ice Cream Truck hit him in the
rear. The front wheels of the hearse were going up in
the air. *Smash! Crash! Crack! Snap!* The hearse was in
two. He and the cab are in the air. Lennie the Shtup
falls into his lap.

The corpse weighs a ton. Down they are coming on
top of the whole traffic mess. Over and over turns the
cab. It drops! Lennie slips from his clutch and slides
into a grave of cabbages. Dan feels for a second the
freedom of angels. They float in the air. Then blood

smacks him in the eyes and he rolls out the torn-away door of the hearse, unconscious.

Let him rest on the asphalt. One foot lies in the open ice cream locker of Foxie's. A popsicle is keeping him cool between the legs.

So let poor Dan rest. In a few months he collects for the heaps that were his Cadillacs. Meanwhile, for a week, he is out of commission in the hospital. Somethin' wrong inside. A little outside too. In the future he don't pee from the same place.

Let Danny lie. Lies around him a gold mine. If only he were up and runnin'. Enough work there is here to put him in the leagues, big, the million-dollar funerals out in Brookline and Newton. But somethin' is missing. This accident will give him pain each time he zips.

And I? Somehow I crossed the Avenue and am goin' around and around a telephone pole on the corner of Talbot Avenue. So I hop out to see what's doin'. Hundreds of cars. What a mess! God has beaten Cadillacs into Fords, hammered Chevrolets into Lincolns. A fender of one attached to a hood of another. A V-8 Pontiac engine revs up in the back seat of an old Crosby. A Plymouth lies on the belly of a Chrysler in a bed of orchids, spinnin' its wheels. A Rambler presses up against an Olds, drools oil on the upholstery. Gasoline and blood smoke on the tar. Yiddish, Italian, Gaelic, Greek . . . angels are singin'. Horns honking. Everybody shoutin', cryin', "Murder, murder!" Ambulances scream. From every hospital in the city they come—Beth Israel, Boston City, Carney; even the State Insane Asylum sends out a car. And watch out. They'll

grab you with a bloody nose. Tow cars! Wreck trucks!
Right and left, they are runnin' over people, lookin' for
customers. Snetsky, our other funeral director, in a
purple convertible hearse, trailing deadly nightshade
from the aerial, wanders about with an eye for work.

Me? I am hoppin' through this junkyard in motion, a
bunch of daffodils in hand: compliments—Lennie the
Shtup. A fender is missin'? I'll take the afternoon off.
After all, how many afternoons will you meet so many
people on the corner of Talbot and Blue Hill? Only on
High Holidays.

Also I am lookin'. I am looking in the dirt and grease,
among the twisted cars and bent people. Where is
Druckman and his horse that made this smash?

I can't see straight. Juices from the fruit wagon spill
over the asphalt. The Avenue steams with the smell of
tangerines and cantaloupes. Honeydew drips into the
sewers. Where a truck full of watermelons fell, rises a
hill of bleeding pulp. The stink of gasoline, the fruit
juices, the hot sun—it makes me dizzy in the head, bad
in the stomach. I sit down.

Somewhere in a melon, maybe I will find a hair of
the Mshulach's beard, a tooth of the horse. Who
knows, under everything perhaps is still a piece of
Druckman's dreck.

Then I see! Would you look for them there? On the
other side of the intersection how did they land? The
five of them are standin' a good one hundred feet clear
of the accident. In the shade of a big potted palm, in

one hundred per cent health, not a scratch, the Cantor is cryin', the Moyhel is weepin', the Mshulach is blowin' his nose. Druckman is dazed. A look on those four pusses, the horse, too—grief, disappointment. With good reason . . .

But that's nothin' to put in an affidavit.

CHAPTER VII

The Saddest Schul

IT WAS the saddest schul I know. The congregation no longer had a building. They rented a basement in the crumbling red-brick two-story which housed Young Israel of Dorchester, a decaying Jewish fraternity still holding on to a few members among the unmarried misfits of Blue Hill Avenue. (How many can that be?) Not that the synagogue had much to do with Young Israel. The balding young men were not of a religious generation. They usually avoided the building around time for services.

Who said though that old men frequented it? Except for High Holidays it was a business to get down in the basement of Young Israel ten adult males requisite for a service. Not a very attractive place to gather—after all, a basement is not designed to be a synagogue.

This one wasn't! Buried up to the windowsills in the earth, there was a foot between the paper-cluttered ground outside and the ceiling of the basement. Two tiny windows with heavy corrugated yellow glass were cramped into this space. They had never, within Young Israel's occupation of the two-story, been open. A little wisp of sunlight now and then would thread into the bleak dark of the cellar. It seeped through a tiny hole in the glass where a beebee pellet had pierced the pane.

Damp, dusty, the basement smelled of old and unwashed clothes. The prayer books were musty and
neglected. Mold was beginning to creep over their
pages. The bindings fell apart when you picked one up.
The daily prayer books were heaped in the same pile as
the holiday machzors. I don't think any of the old men
bothered to use them anyway. They knew the prayers
by heart.

They knew the basement by heart too. Maybe that's
why they didn't come. It was an ache to sit there and
remember the old building where the schul once
stood.

The old schul: there was a temple to be proud of. It
rose, block after block of heavy New Hampshire
granite, on Seaver Street across from the wide, handsome gardens of Franklin Park. An acre of lawn rolled
down from the vast spread of stairs and burst in a
whitecap of flowers along the sidewalk. Here the huge
Doric columns, once a day, threw from the portico the
shadows of their towering crowns.

And inside? A synagogue of marble! A palace among
the lesser schuls of Roxbury, Dorchester, and Mattapan. The ceiling rose so high, your head spun—like
the canopy of the heavens. A breeze of spices hung in
the great space, cinnamon and frankincense. The cedar
of the ark mingled its perfume; while the dull gold of
its hangings shone with soft brilliance in the wide yards
of light that the tall windows brought with the sym-
metry of Arabian geometrics into the hall.

Rich and powerful, our congregation numbered itself
into the thousands, the tens of thousands. It was the

center of orthodoxy in New England. Mayor Curley himself came to lay the cornerstone and auction off the privileges of the schul to the great Jewish magnates of Boston.

What a day! The whole city was there. The Irish Marching Society band blared away. The Ancient Old Honorable Artillery Company banged its guns. Bernie Schloffman and his three combos played morning, noon and night. Senator Lodge made a big speech. Letters, telegrams, contributions, poured in from all over the world: "Congratulations!"—"You should have good luck!"—"What's doing?"

"What's doing?" There wasn't much of an answer in the basement of Young Israel of Dorchester. Of course, most of the temple had moved out to Newton. The synagogue there however was not quite the center of New England Orthodoxy. A sprawling three-acre ranch house, it was no longer Orthodox. Not really Conservative either. Reform? In a way it was. Actually some of the members were already thinking of changing it to Unitarian.

The old schul was sold. It had changed character. Its members moved—to Newton, Brookline, Arlington; all the outlying districts of Boston. What remained of the congregation dispersed to other existing schuls in Dorchester and Mattapan. A handful, however, elected to hold out. This remnant holed up temporarily in the basement of Young Israel for reorganization.

Ten years later they were still in the basement of Young Israel of Dorchester, still in a state of temporary reorganization. The handful had dwindled to one: a combination janitor-rabbi-president-treasurer—let me give you Shammos Yossel Finklestein of Congregation Bnai Tsurris!

"So, what's so funny?" Shammos Yossel would snap, a hand jabbing at his grey beard. It tore at the knot where kinks of tough black hair still grew despite his seventy-two years. Yossel reviewed the situation. What was funny with services about to start, to be standing alone in your Synagogue—staring at the pine-paneled walls? He smashed a fist into his palm.

Pine panels? He had begged them, "Anything but knotty pine panels." Oak, redwood, cedar, straight pine, mahogany—he would pay out of his own pocket the difference. Young Israel was determined though to panel its basement knotty pine, give it a collegiate air. A perfect place it would be to hold intimate little parties and functions. It was the last-ditch effort of Young Israel to retain its youth. And in that last ditch Bnai Tsurris was buried. Who wanted to pray in a play-room? Bad enough all the chairs had to be folded up and stacked against the walls after services. Every day the Shammos kicked the knotholes, hoping to displace a board and gradually get back his bare walls. He gouged his nails into them. Soon they bore more marks than the wailing wall. Some suspected that he scraped off the lacquer with his teeth. Shammos Yossel was a man of anger.

He looked about at the meager possessions of his schul and the pistons of his heart banged up and down with fury. The ark was a portable one, really a suitcase that opened in two. The altar was covered with an

embroidered dish towel, his late wife's. The prayer
shawls hanging by the door looked as if they had just
left her ragbag. Even the covering of the Torah scroll
had so many stitches in it, the velvet looked knotted
with varicose veins.

Blood jumped into his throat. Shammos Finklestein
bit his lips and sucked it back in. Not even a Cantor to
sing! Except on High Holidays you couldn't afford one.
Then came a Cantor. A Cantor? Came Baruch the
Cantor—it hurt your ear to listen; a coughed-out shell
of a voice. His upper register was like squeaking chalk
across a blackboard; his lower, a tubercular spasm. He
didn't sing. He rasped, shouted, clutched at each vowel
and consonant of the Hebrew liturgy and didn't give
them up till he had filled them a few times apiece on
the rusty irons of his vocal chords. On the Day of
Repentance you truly atoned for your sins in the basement of Young Israel.

But every now and then a trace of his former voice
returned. Then the Cantor Baruch's eyes would fill with
tears. You began to cry too. For he would warble for a
second so beautifully, the baritone of his youth filling
the basement with melody—the heavens seemed to
open themselves. Evil lifted from your heart. It fell
away in that single note of hope. Just for a second, as
the old man doubling over the altar in the heavy shroud
of his holiday shawls threw his breast out and made
ready to ascend. Then came the terrible rasp of his age,
chocking the way with blood and phlegm. Again and
again he would try to go up with his voice. Again and
again he fell down to the bowels of spittle and cough-

ing. It was an awful thing to be near. The Shammos shuddered, remembering. His eardrums winced.

For when Baruch cried to be forgiven, he meant it. Not in the distant future, not tomorrow, not even later in the day. "Now," he cried, "forgive me! Now! Why is it taken from me?" he cried on each note. "Give it back—" he shouted, rasped, yelled and screamed. "Give it back!"

Memories haunted the basement of Young Israel. Not even Shammos Finklestein could escape them. He went about in the dark, the electric bulbs screwed off to save money, kicking chairs. One member caught him throwing holy books against the wall. Another, early one afternoon, found him weeping in the corner.

For two years now, he found himself an hour away from minchah, awaiting the before-sundown service, with no congregation. Every morning he prayed that, of their own free will, ten men would come. Every afternoon came no one. It became a matter of the bitterest pride with the Shammos to assemble that minyan. He would take anything male, over thirteen, circumcised, that could lay the remotest claim to being Jewish. One month he even showed up at the State Insane Asylum, trying to get two-hour custody on some of the patients. The congregation had dumped him in this basement to run a synagogue. Let them run! For he would run a synagogue. So they ran. But not to the synagogue.

Shammos Finklestein, however, was not a man without resources. Face to face, an hour before minchah, with an empty pine-paneled room, he did not panic. He didn't fold his hands and sit on them. He turned, eyes gleaming, and walking to the closet—opened the door.

Now I haven't mentioned it before, but the pine-paneled synagogue shared the basement of Young Israel with a large utility closet. This utility closet, filled with brooms, mops and pails of dirty water, had at the back a single window looking out on Blue Hill Avenue.

The Shammos would walk to the back of the closet. He stepped up on an overturned pail. Craning his neck upward, he observed who was walking on the Avenue sidewalk past Young Israel. Heaven forbid, a member of Bnai Tsurris strolled by! The Shammos leaped off his pail. Tripping over mops, brooms, trailing dirty water, he shot up the basement stairs and down the hallway. Hurling himself out the front door and off the porch, he would nab a member of his minyan. Once he had you, that was it. Finklestein's hand gripped you like Death. It was useless to resist.

As a consequence, some people walked fast past Young Israel.

"So what's so funny?"

Excuse me?

"So, what's so funny? Some people walk fast past Young Israel? You think I like it, people should run from me like a boogieman? It suits the dignity of a Shammos, he stands on a pail in a closet and makes eyes at people's legs? It suits my dignity, I got to cry and beg kvetch everyone, come to services? Listen, my friend. Tell everyone—It kills me. Every afternoon before minchah I die a death. When I see a mirror I

spit. I used to be a Shammos. At the old schul up on
Seaver Street I was a Shammos! On High Holidays
millionaires used to come to my door begging—'Give
me a seat.' 'The schul is full,' I'd say, 'no seats. Maybe
for next year I can help you.' So right there in my front
parlor they burst into tears, went down on their knees,
grabbed at my pant legs—'Give me a seat!' With
presents they banged at my door, the wholesale millionaires from the garment district, with blankets,
coats, suits, boxes of underwear, 'Give me a seat!'

"In those days I didn't chase no ten men for a
minyan.

"Go—make with a nasty joke about schuls in the
basement. I used to sit up on the bema in a high silk hat
and a cutaway between the Rabbi and the president at
Seaver Street. When I got up on Rosh Hashanah,
banged my fist on the altar and shouted, 'Will the ladies
in the balcony please be quiet!' you didn't hear no pin
drop. From no one took lip. Give me trouble? I took
you by the seat of the pants and out you went. Once I
threw the colored janitor through the window. Out on
the Seaver Street sidewalk he sat up and learned—don't
thumb your nose at me.

"Never mind—I was a roughneck. To be a shtahkah
is no great thing. I'm not Sampson. In my Talmud,
there I had a little pride. The Torah I knew backwards
and forwards. Often our Rabbi pulled me aside and
checked out a difficult point, waiting—nervous for approval. A Shammos was a scholar.

"Committees I sat on by the dozen; the Building,
Charity, Hebrew School. I was chairman of one, secre-

tary of another, treasurer of a third. Millions of dollars I directed. Fund Raising? With this voice from the bema of Seaver Street I raised ten thousand a night.

"In the community they knew me. Was no one too big to give me the big hello on the street. I walked into a restaurant, the owner himself came out to put the pickle on my plate. Who wants to brag? Once I could keep my mouth shut. Someone else would tell you.

"You think in the basement of Young Israel I had to dig a grave. There I didn't have to get stuck. When Seaver Street moved they begged me, the Rabbi, the Congregation, 'Come out to Newton! You'll be the prince of Shammoses.

"So let me ask you, my friend—Why am I here?

"I want to know, why? I want to know why I'm standing alone every afternoon in a basement schul, staring at dirty walls with pine panels. Why am I chasing up and down Blue Hill among bums, bookies, crooks, looking for a congregation. What am I doing here? Am I crazy?

"Tell me, my friend. Do I need to be a Shammos? Social Security I got. An old-age pension is in my pocket. You want a job? Take it! Do I need tsurris in the basement? So tell me! Tell me! Why I eat my heart out for nothing. Who do I hold onto these prayer books for? For who? For no one! For the dead.

"So what's so funny?"

On the day I was speaking of, Shammos Yossel Finklestein had been standing on one foot on top of a pail, looking out the closet window for over an hour. It

was four P.M. His skull was banging. His parched
mouth pursed and sucked. His tongue curled, its flesh
ribbed like a drying prune. A late afternoon sun bubbled blood in his eyes and broke out in little spots
across his pupils. Finklestein was almost blind from
watching. Blue Hill Avenue swam in patches of light.
Dark pants of old men passing, bright skirts of women
overhead, the gleaming shafts of young girls' legs—all
flowed by like fish. The Shammos swayed, uncertain, on
the pail. Falling forward, he collided with the windowpane.

"Gevult!" Blood dripping from his nose, Finklestein
awoke with a start. "Sukin son sin of a bitch!" the
Shammos swore, Russian and English yoked in vio-
lence. An angry welt swelled on his forehead. Furious,
he drove his fist against the windowpane. An hour!
Not a member had come by. He was sick of looking up
people's legs. The closet was a sweatbox. Under his
arms the skin itched with perspiration. A heat rash of
ugly red spots broke out on his chest. From the cotton
of his underwear, through the linen of his shirt and the
heavy black wool of his rabbinical suit, all of the
Shammos's clothes were soaked. Even the handkerchief
in his pocket went limp, salty and sweaty. His socks
stood in pools of water. His shoes sloshed like swamped
boats.

Where were they? His jewels? Not a single member
sat in the basement. An hour! He attacked the windowpane with his fists. He banged his foot on the pail. The
bottom gave way! Down fell Finklestein, his leg sting-

ing and bleeding, gripped in the sharp edges of a tin vise. Crying with anger, he picked himself up, smashing the pail back and forth across the closet, trying to get loose. It only entangled him more and the slivers of metal gouged long bloody strips down his leg. With a scream he kicked it loose and, enraged, smashed his way out of the closet. Mops, pails, bottles of Lysol, flew in all directions. Up the stairs he limped, hopping and cursing. He would drag ten men down into the basement if he had to kill them first.

Out on the sidewalk, holding his leg in the air, Finklestein danced like a Tartar. He knocked down two ladies and their shopping bags. A dog whirled into the gutter. One of the ladies shouted after him, "You should excuse me." She sat up on the sidewalk on top of a crushed cardboard box of Cheerios. Cornflakes crackled under her skirts. Groceries sprawled everywhere.

The Shammos was deaf to her subtlety. Out on the Avenue he hopped in the midst of a thousand horns, in a swarm of angry drivers. Whizzing by on both sides, they refused to yield. He was trapped between lanes of speeding traffic. Shielding his eyes from the sun, the hopping Shammos peered into the blur of passing cars. It made him weep. Full cars were slipping through his fingers. Jews right and left sped by. They looked down their noses at him. If only they were religious. If only they had a little responsibility. In two minutes he would have a minyan. He could cram the basement full. Jews would be falling out the window. A full schul, it was a box of gold. The Shammos twisted his head to the side. An angry tear ran down his cheek. Fortunes were being lost.

A brake shrieked. The frantic noise of cursing, and in his face an old black Pontiac bleated its horn. The Shammos jumped, jarred from his dream. An inch, and he just missed the loss of a leg. He had wandered to the right. Down the lane of stalled traffic, dirty words came flying at him. Out of the window of the Pontiac, a salesman jammed his head. A puffy red face sucking furiously on a cigar stump, it spit out the stub and jeered, "You in the street! You should sit in your grave. Shmendrick!" The Shammos looked down into his face. He walked up to the Pontiac and lifting his bleeding leg, gave it a kick. A kick! The door buckled.

The Shammos had turned around. Desperate measures were at hand. He hopped toward the curb and jumping onto the sidewalk, ran headlong against the heavy glass doors of Dorchester's chief delicatessen, the G&G.

Immediately half a dozen old men dived under their seats. The rest jumped up and ran fast as hares into the men's room. Dignity, they knew, would restrain Finklestein from too thorough a search. From experience they knew—he couldn't bear the whole G&G should watch him down on his knees searching under tables or begging through the half-open door of the lavatory.

The Shammos searched the G&G. There was no one. Women, children and strangers! No one he knew. Then his eye fell on a sad little figure sitting upright in the corner. One of the faithful remained, Mr. Pfeffer of Aroostook County. Finklestein smiled. He advanced.

CHAPTER VIII

The Shammos from Aroostook County

HALFWAY DOWN the length of the restaurant, Pfeffer sits in a shadow. It is thrown from the air-conditioning unit which juts out of the wall and rises twenty feet off the ground, ten feet from the ceiling. Cheap, harsh, unvaried fluorescent light floods everywhere else. It gleams on the chrome, copper and aluminum behind the counter and on the glass of the display cases piled high with sandwiches. The bright light glares in the aggressive eyes; the chewing, quarreling mouths of the customers are full of it. Only the table where Pfeffer sits is spared a shade of darkness.

Two years before today, Pfeffer crept into this corner and its shadow. Between then and now a few old men had followed him. So he sat there in the company of several others, silent. It was a quiet table. Now and then one old man would say something. Another might answer. But never Pfeffer. Two or three times a day he remarked at the counter: "A cup of coffee," or, "A bagel with cream cheese." At the table, however, he said nothing.

He sat staring at the objects on the table: a sugar bowl, a salt shaker, a pepper shaker, a napkin holder and a glass, usually half-filled, of water. A coffee cup and saucer might be present, or a plate licked clean of cream cheese. These latter objects were quickly removed, though, by the bus boy. So only the bowl, shakers, holder and glass engaged his scrupulous attention. He no longer gave his attention to things that would be taken from him.

Now the Shammos from Aroostook County, locked for hours in silent meditation with a sugar bowl, may appear to you in a bleak aspect. Our perspective would then be at fault. In the head of Pfeffer extraordinary things were doing. He was galloping at that very moment, on a large white horse, sparkling with a diamond bridle, the trusted marshal of the Tsar. Under the flick of Pfeffer's gold baton armies marched across the steppes of Central Asia and Cossack hordes galloped into Lithuania. His white shirt stained with blood, he linked his arm to Trotsky's and shouted to the crowd, "Bread, Chleb and Dreams!" Surrounded by respectful colleagues, Pfeffer gave his considered and deliberate opinion as rector of the Hebrew University of Jerusalem. "It must not be!" Struck by his wisdom, they all agreed.

He moistened his thumb with his tongue. Stuck it in the sugar bowl (his thumb). Withdrew it and sucked. Lonely and despised, and outcast among his brethren— yet half the wealth of the world was his. The railroads of Europe, the ships of the Greeks, the airlines of America, were in his hands. All commerce flowed through Pfeffer's fingers. A gesture of the palm shook the London Exchange. Wall Street rose or plummeted when he clapped. Arbitrary and capricious, his money made money. The world did not love him. Feared and respected, he was the powerful dictator of its fortunes, yet an outcast from its affections. "So, let them despise me! Let them hate me! Let them howl at me!" A tear wetted the Shammos's eye. He dipped a thumb in the sugar bowl. "My wealth," he thought, "is sweet to me."

This had begun two years ago. Six months before that, at the insistence of Lily his daughter, Pfeffer had resigned the one success of his life. He had left a post as Shammos of Aroostook County, Maine, and come to Boston.

The move from Maine was to be a twofold blessing. Pfeffer in the twilight of life would take up residence with a beloved daughter. He would instruct her little seven-year-old, his grandson Heschele, in the aleph-beth of Hebrew.

On some the Almighty beams. On some He never looks. On Pfeffer He smiled once. Woe to the man who counts on continued smiles! A piece of arrogance! Does not the Lord say of the arrogant man, "I and he cannot dwell together in this world?" Poor Pfeffer. His life was salt. Someone dropped him a crumb of sugar. His mouth watered for more.

The elevation to the post of Shammos in Aroostook County had been by sheer luck. Or rather by misfortune. One day he was selling brushes in Dorchester. Not Fuller brushes either. He had already lost a job with the Fuller people. These brushes were part of a wholesale lot a friend had picked up at an auction.

"Peddle them for me, Pfeffer. Take half what you get!" said the friend. "Better still! Who needs them? Give me six bucks—a hundred brushes are yours!"

A hundred brushes? Pfeffer calculated quickly. At fifty cents a brush, they would bring him fifty dollars. Pfeffer was beside himself. A thousand per cent profit! Things like this can snowball. He rushed home to his daughter Lily. "Back me!" he cried. "I'll be Rothschild." She spat in his face. It took an afternoon of wrangling, crying and insulting to wring the six dollars out of her.

The next day Pfeffer set out to sell brushes. The first he sold to Lily. That was a feat King Solomon's merchants couldn't equal. "Brush your hair, wash the woodwork, scrub the toilet. Lily, this brush does everything. A lifetime it lasts!" She paid to get him out of the house. The second one he sold to Lily's landlady, their upstairs neighbor. He had to get down on his knees and clean her kitchen floor to do it. The third went to the blind cripple on the corner. Pfeffer didn't exactly sell it to him. He asked him to hold it for a minute and then took fifty cents out of the collection box. Pfeffer figured that after an hour of holding the brush, the blindeh would get the idea.

A morning of selling! A dollar fifty in his pocket, Pfeffer turned the corner of Lorne Street and headed for the G&G. He was carrying a blue vinyl suitcase stuffed with brushes. It weighed about sixty pounds. The burden was light to him. He had crammed four brushes into his suit pockets. He bulged with brushes like a prospector. Gold dust shone in his expression. A vast syndicate of brushes was opening up before his eyes.

Across the highways of America sped trucks. Barrels of Pfeffer's brushes rattled in them. Rail freight was tied up for months trying to handle the Pfeffer Brush Co., Ltd., account. Ships in the harbors of Boston and New York wallowed under the weight of overseas volume. The longshoremen threw up their hands. In India the underprivileged cried. In Africa the natives grew restless. Pfeffer had to airlift! Millions searched the skies of China, hoping for a brush. And Pfeffer? He sat chain-smoking dark, rich Havanas on top of the Empire State in his penthouse office suite. He watched a plane caper among the clouds. Above the metropolis it spiraled smoke like soap suds and wrote:

PFEFFER: A LIFETIME LAST!

The skirts of his suit puffed with dreams and brushes, Pfeffer was borne quickly toward the G&G. How swift are your feet upon the mountains: O ye Dreamers! Our friend arrived before the doors of the delicatessen. He pushed through them and suddenly the sixty pounds he had been lugging down the Avenue overwhelmed him. Pfeffer's flabby muscles were not used to such weights. Panting, he pushed the suitcase under a table and walked across to the men's room. He was talking business with Rockefeller.

After ten minutes he emerged from conference. A little delicate maneuvering in the men's room and he had gotten rid of certain liabilities. Pfeffer was ready

for new inventory. Sitting down, he put his hand under
the table to pat the suitcase. Nothing! His fingers
clawed the air. The suitcase was missing! Tumbling off
the chair, he was down on his hands and knees under
the table. It wasn't there! Pfeffer tried to control himself. He crawled under all the neighboring tables, looking. Pushing people's legs aside, he searched under
their chair bottoms. Nothing! It was stolen.

Desperate, Pfeffer jumped up. "Who took it?" he
screamed. He ran from table to table, banging so hard
with his fists that the salt and pepper shakers fell over,
shouting in surprised faces, "Who took it?" People
looked at him. "Goniff!" he cried, banging on a table so
hard the sugar bowl jumped. "You crazy?" an old lady
snapped. Pfeffer's head began to whirl. He staggered
back and knocked over one of the busboy's wagons. It
was piled high with dirty dishes. Twenty dollars' worth
of plates shattered on the floor. Pfeffer fled.

Out on the street, a good way down the Avenue,
Pfeffer tried to collect his senses. Highwaymen in the
G&G? Who would do such a thing? (The busboy,
Yanowitz, was even then in the kitchen dumping a trunk
down the garbage chute. A battered blue vinyl trunk
full of dirty brushes—what kind of pig could leave such
a thing?) International Business Thieves! Call in the
FBI? Pfeffer considered. Since Brinks, was there such a
robbery in Boston? And would the police understand?
They know from nothing.

And an immediate problem faced Pfeffer Brush—
Lily! Bankruptcy was impossible. If he didn't come
back with her six bucks, a bed and roof he could kiss

good-bye. Lily's face, that prospect would have driven many a Wall Street broker to the window ledge. Pfeffer began to juggle figures. He had four brushes in his pockets. That was two dollars. He still had a dollar fifty. So his total assets were . . . three fifty. Oy, he was bankrupt. Wait! What if he raised the price of his remaining brushes fifty cents? Is a dollar so much for a brush? Good! So he had—four dollars in inventory, a dollar fifty in cash. Pfeffer, Ltd., was worth five fifty. Not enough! The corporation was climbing from the red. Growth potential was good. Still the stockbrokers clamored. Wait! A switch on the stockholders! The brush he sold Lily—it was in the family. He would just transfer it out of the inactive fund. It would yield a dollar. Six-fifty. He could refund Lily her fifty cents and give her back six dollars. Pfeffer smiled. A little smile. He was in the black.

He had to move fast, however. A trip to Boston's Riviera, Revere Beach, planned for the flush hours of the afternoon, was out. He canceled it. Pfeffer would devote himself to the bread and butter business of selling. A quick sell! Who would take pity on him? Who . . . ? The Rabbi!

Pfeffer turned and began to hurry toward the house of Rabbi Lux in Mattapan. Pfeffer used to work as a janitor in the Rabbi's synagogue. One day, lighting the Sabbath candles, he accidentally set fire to the downstairs chapel. Pfeffer never reported for work again. Rabbi Lux, however, was a man of great kindness. When they met on the Avenue he would greet Pfeffer with a shy smile. Sympathetically he would ask, "When

can you work again, Mr. Pfeffer?" Pfeffer would shake
his head, put his hand on his stomach and show how
sick was the ex-janitor of Rabbi Lux. Indeed, whenever
he saw Rabbi Lux and was reminded of the pews and
ark of the chapel with thousands of books and scrolls
going up in flame, Pfeffer *was* sick.

Now Pfeffer began to tremble in his steps up the
Avenue. He couldn't knock on the Rabbi's door and sell
him an ordinary brush. It was too embarrassing. And
the Rabbi's wife did not possess her husband's forbear-
ance. She would kick him out the door in a minute.
Pfeffer pulled a brush out of his pocket. He looked at
the handle. A plain, unvarnished piece of hardwood,
you could go blind looking for something special. The
brush began to shake in Pfeffer's agitated grasp. He
flipped it over and stared at the bristles. They weren't
nylon. Yet they were too coarse for pig bristle. Some
kind of tough black straw had been hammered in tufts
into the handle. "It's kosher," Pfeffer thought, and his
teeth began to chatter.

Kosher! The word was flame. It set fire to the straw,
the lightheaded part of Pfeffer's brain. He started running along Blue Hill Avenue, talking to himself.
"Kosher! A million brushes are running around. Not a
pig's hair in them. Has one of them been called kosher?
Do the Rabbis call one of them clean? A market! I got a
hundred per cent kosher brush here. I'll go to the
Rabbi. Together we'll look at it. He'll declare it kosher.
He'll give it a blessing. And I'll sell it to him! After him,
the whole community!"

His cheeks afire, Pfeffer mounted the front steps of

the tenement in which the Rabbi dwelt. "Kosher": it
was a gas flame in his head. It made him giddy. A
whole community kosher! He wasn't a businessman. He
was a religious leader. He started stumbling up the
three flights to Rabbi Lux's front door. Pfeffer's temples
worked back and forth, burning. Twice he almost fell
down the steps. Breathing hard, he reached the top
step and flung himself against the door, banging upon it
with the brush, shouting: "Kosher, kosher!"

The Rabbi's wife yanked the door open, frightened.
Pfeffer, caught off balance, fell through the open doorway, flailing a brush, and toppled onto Lux's kitchen
floor, screaming. He was up in a minute. He had a
cramp in his leg or he had sprained it. Around the
kitchen he hopped, shouting, tears of pain in his eyes:
"Kosher, kosher!"

Amazed, the Rabbi's wife backed into a corner and
grabbed a cake knife from the wall. The Rabbi came
out of his study, a scroll in his hand. Pfeffer collapsed
on the kitchen table with his brush, crying. For now he
had begun to cry in earnest.

Tears rolled down his face. Terrible tears, tears of
humiliation and embarrassment. It was agony. God
forbid, a human being should have to weep such tears.
All the foolishness of the morning came up in Pfeffer's
mouth. He was nauseous with pain and disgust. It
spilled out—what had happened the whole morning—
as he beat his head on the Rabbi's table. Every now and
then a word would catch in his throat and then he
would bang with the brush on the table. A dirty brush,
old: Pfeffer wanted to puke when he thought of the

brushes. If he had the suitcase now, he would throw it in the garbage can.

The Rabbi, even his wife, was silent. Before Pfeffer's tears both were embarrassed. The old man's head was going up and down on the formica top of Mrs. Lux's dinette table like a hammer. Suddenly the phone rang. An angel of mercy. "Excuse me, Mr. Pfeffer," the Rabbi said, moving toward the receiver. It was installed directly over the dinette where Mrs. Lux could sit chatting while she chopped cucumbers or beets with her free hand. The cord did not reach into the Rabbi's study. Into the mouthpiece Rabbi Lux, disbelieving, asked the voice that had just spoken into his ear, "From Maine, Long Distance?" Mrs. Lux turned to Pfeffer. "Long Distance, shhhhhhhh!" But Pfeffer was already quiet. The telephone ring had jarred him from hysteria. He blew his nose on his sleeve. Mrs. Lux offered him a napkin. Misunderstanding, he began with the napkin to mop up his tears from the formica.

Little did he know as he blotted tears on the table— at that moment, out of the corner of his eye, the angel of the Lord had caught sight of Pfeffer's life and for a second, with his shy and golden countenance, smiled upon it. The call to Rabbi Lux was from a synagogue in Aroostook County, Maine. There in the northernmost reaches of the United States, among tall pines and streams of running crystal, a little congregation was in need of a Shammos. Could the Rabbi help, they wanted to know. Nobody wanted to come up so far away from Boston. "We don't need much," they told Rabbi Lux. The schul was small. It didn't take much to keep it up.

"We need someone who knows a little Hebrew. Can lead a service. Sing. (He doesn't need to be Caruso.) He'll teach the children on Sundays. And if he doesn't know everything, it's all right. Let him fake a little." Rabbi Lux looked down at Pfeffer.

"Rabbi!" the voice continued on the phone. "Let him fake a little. He's doing us a favor. Who will come and be our Shammos? We got no one. It's a mitzvah. Send someone! I'll kiss his face every morning. Rabbi, let someone take pity on us!"

"Wait a second," said Rabbi Lux. He put the receiver down on the kitchen table. The Rabbi walked over to Pfeffer, who had hidden his face in his hands and was breathing painfully. Rabbi Lux put his hand gently on Pfeffer's shoulder and asked softly, "Mr. Pfeffer, can you work again?"

So Pfeffer became a Shammos in Aroostook County. He was received with great respect by the congregation. The Rabbi said over the telephone, "I'm sending a good friend of mine to you." A friend, a good one, of Rabbi Lux, the great Talmudist of Mattapan! The congregation expected another Rashi to dwell in their midst. Pfeffer did not entirely disappoint them. He could pinch his nose like a scholar. He coughed in a very learned manner. When he scratched his head you could swear he was thinking something very deep. In short, Aroostook County was delighted with its Shammos.

From house to house went the Shammos of Aroostook County for a whole month. In each family, whether the meal was breakfast, supper or brunch, the table was set out for a banquet. The father clapped him on the back, the mother lavished attention on his every need, the children crowded around his chair waiting to have their cheeks pinched.

"Reb Pfeffer," booms the head of the household, "you got a generous congregation. About asking, don't worry." A husky hand slipped a twenty-dollar bill into Pfeffer's back pocket.

"More herring, Rabbi Pfeffer?" complains the wife. "You don't eat." With challah, fruits and nuts, the Shammos's mouth was crammed. With honey his lips were stuck together. What could he say?

Pfeffer, for once in his life, was shrewd. He said nothing. When the men started to engage him in conversation about a point of Law or an interpretation of the Torah, he kept quiet. He would smile blissfully to show how it pleased him that such things concerned them. If pressed, he would shake his head in a way that, as the observer wished, could be interpreted yes or no. And if really pushed, Pfeffer put his finger to his cheek. "Of that I never thought!" he exclaimed. Suddenly he would wink at his interrogator. What a wink! It was full of mischief and delight. It seemed to say, "Ah, you are a clever one to come up with such a question. The great Rabbis themselves never thought of it. With such a smart fellow what shall I do?"

So flattered would the questioner be by the Shammos's wink, inevitably he forgot what he had asked.

So Pfeffer throve in Maine. The synagogue was a beautiful one. It had been built of wood. Cedars were cut in the surrounding forest. Maple and oak were hewn down for the beams. The boards were pegged together and not a nail had been driven into the building. Nor was there any electricity. The synagogue had a huge skylight which poured light, even on the darkest day, through the length and breadth of the room. Candleholders stood by every pew for evening services. It was a custom that each family brought its own candles. Often they brought candles of bayberry. The schul, however, had a spice of its own. The naked wood was sweet and clean. Not a board had been painted. Even when the ceiling had been put on inside, the synagogue it smelled like an open space.

The congregation had built the synagogue with their own hands. One of their number was a lumber dealer who had started his business twenty years before in the forests with only the clothes on his back and an axe. He carved the Ten Commandments into the doors of the ark. Like timber markings that showed the boundaries of a man's rights, the Hebrew letters stared large and honest at the congregation. When the scrolls were drawn out of the cedar chest they smelled as if they had been wrapped around the trees. The congregation crowded forward to touch the parchment with the ends of their prayer shawls. They prized their synagogue, simple and open. Lumbermen and potato farmers, a few storekeepers and a springling of tailors, the congregation and Pfeffer got along well.

He lived in a little house just behind the synagogue. Here he cooked and slept. The congregation wanted to hire a servant for him; Pfeffer said no. He would be happier taking care of himself. Duties were light. Fridays and Saturdays he conducted services. On holy days and when someone died and the mourners wanted to bring the coffin by, Pfeffer opened the schul. Otherwise he loafed. He walked through the woods. He slept. He got into the station wagon the congregation had given him and drove into a little town nearby to have a cup of coffee or a meal in its single restaurant. That is all he did. That is, except for Sundays.

Sunday came the children. All week Pfeffer would daydream and scheme for the event. Sunday morning a throng of wild, screaming children came running and pushing into the synagogue to attend their weekly class at Hebrew School. From three years old to twelve, they scrambled and fought under the pews and up and down the aisle. (The boys who were approaching thirteen were sent down to Bangor on a special bus to be trained by the Rabbi for Bar Mitzvah.) For half an hour Pfeffer tried to teach them Hebrew. Not that Pfeffer knew much Hebrew. He could teach them to read the alphabet. He was skillful in translating several pronouns such as you, he, she, me, I and it. One or two songs he knew by heart. Ah, I forgot! He sent them home knowing how to construct some of the most important sentences in the Hebrew Grammar. For instance: "I love Mother." "I love Father." "I love brother." "I love sister." What more does any Jewish parent want?

No, Pfeffer did not tax them with more than they could absorb. What did he do with the rest of the time? The first morning the Shammos had really been worried. In half an hour he had exhausted his stock of

knowledge in the Hebrew vernacular. They were beginning to shift in their seats. A disaster would follow if
he made them read from the prayer books. It wasn't a
small room. You couldn't keep your eye on sixty children and correct the pronunciation of whoever was
reading. Pfeffer wasn't too sure of the pronunciation
himself.

"I'll introduce myself," thought Pfeffer, "and let them
go home early." He said, "Good morning children."

"Good morning, Mr. Pfeffer!" they echoed back,
wondering what he was up to.

"You know it's a pleasure to see so many Jewish children together. Such things couldn't happen when I was
a little boy."

The jostling in the seats stopped. "Why?" a tiny voice
asked from the pews.

"Oy," said Pfeffer, leaning forward on the bema and
pulling at his nose, "used to come on horses the Cossacks and chase the Jews if too many got together."

Silence suddenly filled the syngagoue. "What's a Cossack?" a shrill shout in the back inquired.

"God forbid you should ever see one!" Pfeffer whispered. He leaned toward the children. "A Cossack was
an outlaw, specially trained to hate the Jews. A big
sword he used to carry between his teeth, and under a
fur cap he shaved his head naked. Like you and me he
didn't eat. He didn't eat kosher. Little children and
dogs he used to eat. The only thing he wouldn't touch
for supper was his horse."

"Did you ever see one?" a little girl asked.

"Did I ever see one?" said Pfeffer, pretending to be

annoyed. "Used to come a Cossack and chase me home from Hebrew School every day."

So, Pfeffer started telling them stories. That morning he told them how he had led his schoolfellows to ambush a band of one-eyed Cossacks in the Hebrew School backyard. How he, a little boy, had shot the king of the Cossacks with a silver bullet.

"What a Cossack was the king! The skulls of pigs hung from his saddle. His nose was red and bumpy like a bunch of cherries. Black curly hair came pouring out of his nose, his ears, his mouth, and ran wild all over his face. He used to stick out a white tongue that was four feet long. He would murder people just with his awful laugh."

The Shammos began to laugh, a low, malicious chuckle that echoed up and down the synagogue, sending a tingle down the children's spines. His eyes glittered. A little girl in the first row began to cry. Pfeffer stopped. His face relaxed and he smiled affectionately at the audience. "Well, that's what the king of the Cossacks was like."

Then to cheer up the little ones, he told the story of the Tartar who cut off his uncle Lutkie's nose. He was describing the wanderings of poor Lutkie through the steppes of Siberia to get his smell back, when twelve o'clock struck and it was time for the spellbound children to go home.

The next Sunday the Shammos finished with Lutkie. What accidents befall a man who can not sniff! Especially in Russia.

He began to tell them of his great-grandmother

Shaindele; Shaindele the great and her golden couch.
"Imagine a woman of two hundred who looks like a girl
of sixteen. And wise beyond her years. Why, from all
over the world came Rabbis and scholars to lie where
she lay. Why? She reclined on the sofa that belonged to
the Queen of Sheba."

Sunday after Sunday the Shammos drew up stories
from the well of his inexhaustible imagination. They
came up from a life that had been filled with day-
dreams. How they spilled out of the Shammos! He
would prance around the platform, imitating a man
without a nose trying to smell his barley soup. He put
his finger, his tongue, his ear in the soup, till the children started howling so with laughter that he had to
stop for fear they'd hurt themselves. Then he bent over
confidentially and told them how he had saved the city
of Drozhky from starvation with a magic potato. Yes, it
was he, little Pfeffer, running down the main street of
Drozhky trying to hide the potato under his blouse
from hungry eyes. If the Rabbi blessed it three times
with the Shema Yisroel, it would multiply. Like God it
would be one, but one found everywhere. But a crowd
was chasing him. They smelled the potato. They were
greedy to gobble it up. Who would believe him? It was
a mile to the Rabbi's!

Pfeffer began to walk through the woods around the
schul. There he would rehearse the plots he intended to
spin out the coming Sunday in Hebrew School. Afternoons would find him wandering along forest paths,
dawdling and dreaming, as he had dawdled and dreamt

as a little boy in the forests of White Russia outside his town.

Among the sugar maples through which threaded the tiny footpath, Pfeffer would suddenly hear a crash in the underbrush. It was Malke, the Rabbi's enchanted goat.

"Malke, Malke!" the Shammos called timidly, taking a few steps toward the noise. A shape immediately burst through the bushes and arose on the wing far above his head.

"Malke, why do you fly away?" the Shammos called after it. It was too late. The goat had changed into a bird. Only the Rabbi of Drozhky could summon the animal back. Oh yes, Pfeffer knew the Rabbi's goat. As a little boy he used to peep through the slats of the Rabbi's fence at Malke. The goat often winked at him. They had an understanding. Often in the woods the little boy could hear Malke treading leaves behind him. It was Malke who threw the wolves off his trail. Malke led him home when he got lost. As the Rabbi's wife would say, "It's magic. A gallon a day? Either that or it's crazy!" Pfeffer and his unseen companion had many adventures together. In league they had saved the village of Drozhky from many disasters it never even suspected. What was Malke doing in America? Thought the Shammos, "Maybe it's a niece?"

The woods were full of experiences for Pfeffer. Once, taking a nap in a grove of pines, he awoke to hear a low voice calling his name, whispering from the ground. Opening his eyes, he saw Lilith, Queen of Satan, smiling at him. Too frightened to move, the Shammos lay upon the ground. Lilith slipped in among the trees. The pines began to melt with her desire. Beads of pitch oozed out along their branches, and in the heady smell Pfeffer almost fainted. The tops of the trees swayed above his head. A warm wind touched his cheek. The branches brushed against each other. They moaned. Cones came tumbling down. Between two trees Lilith's body appeared. She brushed away green gauze from her shape and putting her long, slender hands under her white breasts, showed them to the Shammos. "Aaaaaahhh" she whimpered. He trembled. The nipples grew hard and swelling, wiggled at him. Turning around, she wiped away the film from her behind and made her buttocks shake. They glowed with a rosy blush. A little flame licked between her legs. It beckoned him like a tongue. He felt her coming closer. A finger crept up his leg. "Fire! Fire!" screamed the Shammos. He jumped up and ran. The trees teetered as he fled along the path. A black shape loped toward him. It was a wolf with green, glittering eyes. Stopping five feet away, it laughed, and then sprang for Pfeffer's throat. "Shema Yisroel!" shouted Pfeffer, grabbing for its neck. He had hold of the wolf and throttled it. Baring yellow teeth, it snarled furiously, struggling. He spit in its eye. Slinging the wriggling body over his shoulder, the Shammos smacked it against a tree and broke its spine. Then grabbing the carcass by the tail, he hurled it into the bushes and sped homeward. This was one of the stories he didn't tell in schul.

The forest was usually kinder. There was one clearing where Pfeffer often lay. It was a lawn of wild daisies and blue forget-me-nots. Here he remembered the dreams of his childhood. A bumblebee would buzz overhead and he dozed off into the romances of a ten-year-old boy. Pfeffer the Rabbi of Poland; Pfeffer, the secret partner of Herzl; Pfeffer, successor to Zola; Pfeffer, confidant of Rothschild; on and on went his brain, ceaselessly turning up possibilities. He published a newspaper that turned out articles about himself.

Social

Moses Montefiore Entertained His Good Friend Mr. Pfeffer Today upon His Steam Yacht in the Harbor at Odessa

Financial

Tsar Begs Pfeffer To Purchase the Suez

and *Political*

PFEFFER CARRIES UNITED STATES, RUSSIA AND CHINA, FIRST JEWISH PRESIDENT OF THE WORLD

Some of the lesser of these fantasies the Shammos communicated to the children. For instance, how he built the Warsaw-to-Pinsk railroad.

This was not entirely false. Pfeffer had indeed helped to lay the track out of Warsaw, driving spikes twenty miles toward Pinsk with his own arms. He only exag-

gerated his role. Also he omitted to mention that he had
been fired for laying three miles of track upside down.
The Shammos, however, never told an outright lie.
Until he was kicked out of cheder for dreaming at his
desk, he had seriously intended to enter the rabbinate.
Who knows, with more sympathetic instructors he
might as well have become the grand Rabbi of Poland.
And Pfeffer's liason with Herzl was no fiction. He had
gone out collecting with a little box for Zionism several
times. Was it his fault he forgot to turn it in? Otherwise
he probably would have so distinguished himself in collecting that a rapid rise in the Zionist hierarchy would
have been inevitable. Didn't Pfeffer once write obitu-
aries for the Drozhky *News?* Even Zola had to start
somewhere. Even Zola could make a mistake like con-
fusing the births with the deaths. Mr. Rothschild! You
once employed Pfeffer. You or your agents in Drozhky
bonded him as a runner for the bank. So he dropped the
envelope. So he lost it. So?

The children recognized in Pfeffer's stories that quality which separates great men from fools—Imagination.
They admired in him a sense of life which leads men in
the midst of poverty, bad luck and disaster, to hope.
Uncorrupted by adult minds, the children did not
crassly distinguish between ideas and their realization
in the hazardous bustle of an everyday world. The success of a great man did not depend for them upon his
visible material achievements. You have all seen the
slogan of the latter point of view. It hangs on the greasy
walls of flea-bitten diners and in the dusty lobbies of
third-rate hotels. "If you're so smart, why ain't you

rich?" The truly wealthy never subscribe to it. They know how capricious is the credit of the note in their hand. They always hear in their ears the malicious clink of the rolling dice. They would have appreciated Pfeffer, taken him into their arms as a brother. "Pfeffer!" Rockefeller would have said, "You're such a dreamer!" and affectionately have pinched his cheek.

For Pfeffer was a great man. The children sensed in him the earnestness and excitement of a genius. Was it his fault that bad luck plagued him? He was a shlimazzel. Did he ask for bad luck? It came to him.

Ah, you amateur psychologists. I hear you grumbling. "What's this came to him? Of its own accord bad luck came to him? Does bad luck get up on its legs, stroll up to a fellow, tap him on the shoulder and say, 'Excuse me, I'm with you?' "

"If this Pfeffer had bad luck," you say, "he was looking for it. He didn't really want to succeed. He willed himself into failure. In short, what he got, he was looking for."

This, my dear psychologist, may explain why you lose a letter or a pin. However, how about a whole life which Coincidence thumbs its nose at? Yes, I speak of Coincidence as a person, a malicious one. It placed Pfeffer at the right time in the right place talking to the wrong person. It had a lady friend too, Bad Luck. And the two lay awake at night, tickling each other in bed, hatching evil for Pfeffer.

And perhaps you are right. What if Pfeffer *did* will himself to fail? Think of the amount of failure he endured. It required the constitution of a horse to swallow the measure of embarrassment and humiliation which he gulped down in an average week. You know he didn't just lie down and take it. When Bad Luck and Coincidence sat on his doorstep in the morning, waiting, he didn't hide in the hallway. He opened the front door and walked out quickly, pretending not to see them. Halfway down the street, they caught up and the fight began. He wrestled with them across front lawns, kicking over milk bottles and tripping schoolchildren, struggling until they had knocked him into the gutter. Jacob had an easier time of it wrestling with the angel. And when, defeated, thrown in his first match, his hat crushed under a car, his shirttail torn, Pfeffer picked himself up, dusted off his coat, retrieved his chapeau, stuffed his shirt back in, smiled and walked sprightly on his way—who could deny he was a hero? His life was a tragedy. He tried to breathe and he hoped.

So poor Pfeffer was a great man. He suffered continual misfortunes. The number of these misfortunes gives them magnitude. Yet he struggled against them. What can we conclude? Pfeffer is a tragic hero. He is also a shlimazzel.

Like all tragic heroes, Pfeffer was guilty of hubris. He was shrewd enough with the congregation. He never got up at Friday night service to tell the members how he had saved the whole of Poland with a magic potato. In Maine he knew his limits. However in his letters to Lily in Boston, the Shammos could not resist expanding a little.

"Dear Miss Pfeffer," he began them. Pfeffer delighted in the formality his position allowed him. He also delighted, though he would not admit it to himself, in addressing his daughter as Miss Pfeffer. It was a sharp reminder to her that the child she had borne was illegitimate. Pfeffer always drove this point home by beginning each epistle after that salutation with the concerned question—"How is your little Heschele?" Then the Shammos would begin to enumerate the many honors and responsibilities that the congregation had heaped on his shoulders in the past week, and how many they planned to heap in the coming one. This way he got to tell Lily about them twice and could engage both in speculation and evaluation as to their importance. And large as they loomed in foresight one week, they were always sure to grow a good deal in hindsight the next. "Well, I'm Chairman of the Building Committee. Have I got my hands full with plans and blueprints." So the next week: "The Annex is going up. I'm rushing things. You know lumber, the price goes up every day. Two cents a foot in the last month. This way we save a fortune. The president of the synagogue, a millionaire, says I got the business sense. I should run a construction company, he tells me." And the next week: "Have I been busy! The president of the synagogue has to run around like an office boy for me. I pulled a deal on the lumber. Oy Lily, you would be proud of me. Did I pull the wool over their eyes in the Bangor lumberyards. Then here I had to fight with the carpenters, masons, plumbers . . . the whole lot. (Overtime I've been getting from them for nothing. I should be Secretary of Labor.) But with God's help it's almost finished. I inspected every corner of it from top to bottom." Thus was the Shammos's new outhouse reported in Boston.

You can imagine how Pfeffer's prowess as a Shammos, a scholar, a Hebrew teacher and community leader, grew as the months fled by. His letters had the desired effect upon Lily. Perhaps too much so. He had been smart. Too smart! He started small. Letter by letter, his stature began to grow. So Lily swallowed everything. She believed in the reports as if they were Holy Script. She told the neighbors, upstairs, downstairs and across the street. She told half of Dorchester. And while the Shammos repeated his exploits twice in two weeks, Lily repeated them twice every two hours. If Pfeffer had to dream, Lily had to talk.

Her replies to the Shammos began to change. Lily never wrote letters. She answered Pfeffer's with postcards. The salutations of these missives underwent a subtle variation of melody. They tripped down the musical scale from "Listen, Pfeffer!!" to "Pfeffer!" to "Mr. Pfeffer" to "Dear Pfeffer" and "Dear Father" and finally to "Papa."

The Shammos began to warm toward his only daughter, his child Lily. Who else did he have in the world? Mrs. Pfeffer had jumped off the Custom House tower twenty years ago. Like her mother, Lily was highstrung. You had to forgive her for a temper tantrum now and then. Pfeffer forgave. He pushed out of his mind a number of unpleasant memories. The times she locked him out of the house. The day she reported him to the police as a vagrant. The occasion on which she attempted to have him committed to the State Insane

Asylum. (An Inspector came over to the house to talk with Pfeffer, but as Lily strode up and down the kitchen screaming, trying to goad her father into showing a little anger, the Inspector began to show more interest in her.) Pfeffer was of a generous nature. He forgot! Lily also forgot. Not that she was of a generous nature. She just forgot.

Three years went by. Pfeffer was still in Maine. Suddenly a note of urgency sounded in Lily's postcards. "Papa, little Heschele is having trouble in Hebrew School. Take a vacation! Come home." And, "What shall I do? Heschele is falling behind. He needs special teaching." Finally, "Don't strain in Maine! Retire. We love you here. Heschele needs your help."

Pfeffer exaggerated truth. Lily disregarded it. Heschele's trouble in Hebrew School had nothing to do with falling behind. He was a complex little boy. . . . However.

Maine was lonely. The Shammos longed for a cup of coffee with his old cronies on Blue Hill Avenue. The thought of retiring into the bosom of his daughter's affection appealed to him. Pfeffer was lonely for a little filial warmth. After all, who loves you like your family?

He gathered from his daughter's postcards that her Heschele wasn't too bright. Good! He could apply the teaching methods he had perfected in Maine. Lily had told the whole neighborhood about him. Maybe he would take on a few pupils of similar aptitude. He could run a little school in Dorchester. His daughter would fawn upon him. Pfeffer decided to go.

Of all the dreams he ever dreamed . . . Let us skip over a few pages, the reception at North Station, a neighborhood banquet, his speech on Hebrew Education to the Beth-El Breakfast Club. Let us go directly to Mr. Pfeffer's first lesson with his grandson.

The boy was unusually silent through the first week of his grandfather's return. Amid the festivities no one noticed it. When Pfeffer departed for Aroostook and the woods, Heschele was coming out of babyhood, taking off diapers and putting on underwear. Lily had kept her father away from the baby. She threatened to push his teeth down his throat if she caught him tickling it or pinching its cheek. So Pfeffer avoided the cradle. Once, it is true, when the refrigerator was empty of milk, he had taken the warm formula from his tiny grandson's fingers. Who remembers such things?

"Good morning, Heschele!" the Shammos exclaimed, beaming with delight on his eight-year-old grandson. It was Monday morning, a week after his arrival. He had just walked into the dining room, where the cloth had been removed and books piled onto the oak top of the table in preparation for the beginning of their lessons. The Shammos's cheeks were as rosy and red as pickled pears. The taste of fruit juice was in his mouth. His countenance overflowed with confidence. "Good morning, Heschele!" he repeated, making his way to the chair at the head of the table. Heschele did not reply but got up from a seat in the middle of the long table and walked to one at the foot of the board, where he sat down. He eyed his grandfather.

"Good morning?" the Shammos asked. He put it like

a question. Heschele said nothing. Pfeffer gave a little laugh. The boy's reticence amused him. Perhaps he was retarded? So much the better.

Pfeffer pulled a Hebrew primer from the stack of books. "Today, Heschele," he said, smiling indulgently, "we'll try a few letters from the Hebrew alphabet; then if you're good I'll tell a story." He smiled hugely on his grandson. The little boy's face was tense with emotion.

"Aleph," the old man intoned, slowly and distinctly.

"Aleph, beth, gimel, daleth," the little boy shouted, galloping like a mad horse through the letters of the Hebrew alphabet. On the last one, tov, he stopped short, his nostrils quivering.

Mr. Pfeffer looked down the table at his little grandson Heschele. On the back of his neck a pimple began to prickle. A pair of green eyes stared at him. Pfeffer swallowed. "Pretty good, nu, pretty good," he stammered, rubbing his nose and looking down at the table. What would he do next?

"Let's conjugate!" a little voice piped from the bottom table.

Pfeffer looked up surprised. Already the little one knew conjugation? A teacher, however, has to keep the upper hand. He drew the wrinkles of his mouth into a condescending and long-suffering amusement.

"Well," he said, shaking his finger, "let's not go too fast. Haste makes waste. God took seven days to make the Universe. He could have just batted an eye. A pickle doesn't pickle in a day. We could try the verb to love."

"Ohev, ohavti, eh—ehav." Heschele ran through the present, past and future tenses like a soda clerk reeling off flavors. A silly grin twitched on Pfeffer's lips. The past he was shaky on. The future he wasn't even sure existed.

Mr. Pfeffer looked down the table. Two fishy little eyes glared at him. A bone stuck in the Shammos's throat. He began to cough.

"Why don't *you* conjugate?" the little voice called alluringly to him.

Pfeffer cleared his throat. He brought his fist down on the table and declared firmly, "Time for Hebrew history!

"Once upon a time . . ." the Shammos began. Silence from the end of the table. Pfeffer relaxed and softened his tone. ". . . there was a man called Adam and a lady called . . ."

A thin little staccato voice recited from the end of the table: "In the beginning God created the heaven and the earth. Now the earth was unformed and void, and darkness was upon the face of the deep; and the Spirit of God hovered over the face of the waters. And God said . . ."

"Excuse me, I got to go to the men's room," said the Shammos. He got up and rushed out of the room. A few minutes later Lily came in. Heschele was told that grandfather wasn't feeling good. Tomorrow morning they could make up what they had missed. The son smiled mockingly at his mother.

The next morning the Shammos entered the dining room with something less than a jaunty air. He was pale. From his cheeks the juice had been squeezed. He didn't greet his pupil with a "good morning," but sat down quickly and announced in a peremptory voice that today they would concentrate on reading from the Hebrew prayer book. Pfeffer assigned a page. Heschele obediently began to drone. The Shammos settled back in his seat and closing his eyes, began to nod. Bad dreams had kept him up all night. Now perhaps he could steal a nap. The Hebrew rose and fell musically. Camels jogged across his brain. Seated between the humps, he bumped back and forth pleasantly in a caravan of Solomon crossing the Sinai. Silks and oranges, musty scrolls, the goods sent up a pleasant perfume that lulled him to a deeper sleep.

Suddenly a voice hawked in his ears, "What does it mean?"

"Eh?" said Pfeffer, shaking his head.

"What does it mean!" the voice screeched.

Through the heavy curtains of his eyes the Shammos saw two little green bugs crawling toward him. He snapped his head and awoke to see little Heschele, his neck craned forward and his eyes glittering, shouting from the other end of the table.

"What does it mean?" Pfeffer's grandson shouted again, his face red.

"What?" asked the Shammos.

"The Hebrew!" Heschele screeched. And he repeated a sentence from the text. Pfeffer was confused. He couldn't even find the place. He shrugged his shoulders. "Conjugate the verb 'to speak'!" Heschele demanded.

The Shammos was confounded. "Decline the noun 'father.'"

Distraught, Pfeffer cried angrily, "Who's teaching who?"

"Don't pick your nose," Heschele shot back.

Pfeffer's hand came down from his nostril, trembling. "You are a fresh little . . ."

"Bastard!" Heschele put in. "I am a bastard."

"I got to go to the bathroom," the Shammos said.

"Don't pee in your pants!" the little boy cried after the fleeing form of his grandfather.

For two days, Wednesday and Thursday, the Shammos lay in bed except for meals. At the table Lily said nothing. Pfeffer could feel the anger bubbling under her apron. She slammed his plate down and dished out his portion as if it were dirt. Heschele had poisoned his bread.

Pfeffer wanted to cry. He bit his lip and held back his tears. He couldn't go back to Maine. He resolved to try once more. Thursday night he announced at supper that the following morning, before the Sabbath, he would teach a lesson.

All night Pfeffer sat on his bed cramming. He leafed desperately through Hebrew grammars, prayer books, copies of the Talmud and the Torah. Nothing would stick. It never had before. Why should it now? His mind was a panic-stricken blank. Occasionally a proverb scrawled against it: "The ass opens its jaws and brays, a wise man keeps his mouth shut." About four in the morning, the lights still on, Pfeffer fell back against the pillow, tearing his hair. Nothing! He knew nothing! He cupped his face in his hands and began to weep. His tears turned into snores. In a few minutes he was mercifully asleep.

Pfeffer woke up. His cheeks were wet. He lay as he had as a boy in the dew and grass, sleeping in the fields outside Drozhky. The sun poured through the window and blazed on the pillow. The innocence of mornings long ago took hold of him. A hot sun rose out of the red rim of dawn and called: "Turn thyself to the world." Under the awakening light, the rooftops of Drozhky blazed like fiery bushes. He jumped up and shook the rain from his hair. Drozhky was on fire in the distance. Pfeffer lifted himself on his elbows in the bed. The world, the krassavitza, stretched before him. Oy! He could laugh with life.

Then he remembered the task he had set himself that morning. The dew turned to brine. He tasted the bitterness of his pillow. Drozhky was extinguished in the dusk. The Shammos crawled out of bed, put on his clothes and like an ox to the slaughter, staggered down the hall to the dining room.

Heavily, he fell into his chair. The flesh tightened along his throat, waiting for the sharp little voice. Silence? Pfeffer looked up. Heschele was smiling at him. The boy's hands were neatly and respectfully folded on the table. An apple sat by Pfeffer's place.

"Good morning, zaide!" Heschele called out cheerfully to his grandfather. Pfeffer blinked. He couldn't believe it.

"Good morning, zaide!" Heschele called out again.

Pfeffer was dumbfounded. He couldn't speak. What was this?

"Zaide," the little boy called, lingering affectionately over the Yiddish. "Zaaaide," he bleated, "you promised to tell me a story."

Pfeffer looked at his little lamb. "You wasn't such a good boy." The remark dropped with suspicion from his lips. Heschele said nothing. He looked at his grandfather. The little boy's eyes were hazel now. Innocence shone in them. They appealed to the Shammos for a story. Hope puckered Heschele's lips. Penitence pinched his chin. Such a sweet face! Despite himself, the Shammos began to relent. "A story?" he asked quizzically.

"A story about yourself!" the little boy suggested eagerly.

Pfeffer looked at his grandson. The child's face was earnest. Pfeffer sighed. He replied, "Whatever happened to me? Nothing!"

"Not even when you were *little?*" Heschele begged. The Shammos eyed his grandson. The boy's face was earnest and open. Not a trace of malice was to be seen. Only a shade of disappointment was beginning to cloud his hazel eyes. He pursed his tiny lips sadly. Pfeffer was touched.

The Shammos leaned back in his chair. He picked up a prayer book from the pile in front of him, blew the dust off the cover and rubbed the binding under his nostril. He could sniff the age of the book. It brought back a thousand memories of his days in the cheder of Drozhky. It seemed as if the whole purpose of his life as a child had been to skip cheder. To get lost in the woods, or get sent on an errand in the opposite direction, a few minutes before it began. He had been out of school more than in it through the course of those years. Yet the drone of Hebrew that put him to sleep in the back of the classroom or set him to carving his desk had not entirely escaped him. Stories stuck in his mind. Little legends and anecdotes from the Bible silently crept into his imagination and filled his dreams with figures, strange, often haunting. He would climb to the top of a hill and, like David, yearn toward Jonathan fleeing. Slinging a stone at a giant oak he would topple Goliath. On the cliffs overlooking the Pina River he watched the waters divide, then rise up and overwhelm a strange host of chariots. Once in the forest he heard a trumpet and the angel Gabriel stood before him for a second, smiling.

"Well . . ." said the Shammos, leaning back in his chair, lost in these memories. "Once something strange happened." He rubbed the siddur under his nose, smiling to himself.

"When I was a little boy? Oy! I wasn't such a good one myself. I wasn't always in cheder. I was always missing. Half the town spent their time looking for me. Outside Drozhky, my town, there was a field of tall grass. Grass so high, a man could ride through on a horse—it was over his head. I used to hide in that grass. I would lie on my back between the tall blades and look at the sky, thinking. What did I think about? Everything! I thought about God and the Universe, I rolled my head back and back before anything was created and rolled it forward and forward to what would happen and happen. I used to get faint and dizzy thinking. I used to think about Drozhky, my town, of dirt streets, wooden houses that fell down, goats and sheep running through its alleys, the men knocking each other down in the synagogue, our Rabbi a drunk. Drozhky wasn't Jerusalem.

"Lying in the grass, I would think about death. When I was three the angel of darkness beat his wings in my house. The next morning my mother lay stiff in her room. My father, your great-grandfather, was a chicken plucker. His fingers were always full of feathers. Also he was always coughing. The down made him sneeze. He got sicker and sicker and finally had to bring the chickens home with him. He lay in bed, coughing, sneezing, running a fever and plucking chickens. When I stayed in the house I began sneezing too. So I would sleep in the fields.

"I used to think about this world; about the countries beyond Poland and Russia; about America across the big ocean, where my cousins had gone. The buildings were made with bricks of gold; in the streets were silver cobblestones. What they didn't write! Who cared? I flew across the world. I would make a bridge from Poland to America and then to Jerusalem. I saw the beams stand up in the grass. I tied together continents.

"I remember my last year in Drozhky. The cholera came. The scarlet fever came. The chicken pox and the measles ran through town. Every disease in the book dropped into Drozhky to kill a few people. My father stopped plucking chickens in his bed. He lay back in the sheets and coughed like a rooster with laryngitis. I was afraid to go near him.

"Everybody was dying. The peasants got angry and began to steal and set fires. Even the Cossacks were sick. Their horses fell down in the street, and they ran out of taverns with green spots on their faces. The whole town was crazy.

"So I slept in the grass. I could grab an armful and fall on it whenever I wanted. It tickled. It scratched your cheek. The earth that was hard, it made soft. Every night I dropped into it. In the grass I could have lived forever, running after birds, grabbing turtles, pulling out fish from the ponds and making dreams.

"What did I start to say? Oy, something strange that happened. It was so long ago, I'm not sure now. One morning I woke up like you fall out of bed from a bad dream. Sweat is on my face. I sat up in the grass. The sky looks like cherry juice. It's autumn but the air is hot. The sun is still under the hills, but they are red too. I looked to Drozhky. It's burning! Flames are everywhere. The grass at the edge of the field is catching fire. Gott! I'm frightened. My town, my grass is disappearing.

"I can't breathe. The world is smoke. My eyes sting. In the grass all the birds are crying. My eyes can't see. Down in Drozhky terrible things are happening. I can hear the screams of women. The Cossacks are loose. My father is dying. Oy, Papa! What can I do? They'll kill him. He'll burn in his sheets full of feathers. My father! Oy, Papa, Papa . . .

"I'm running to Drozhky and a voice shouts, 'Pfeffer!'

It's a mistake? I stop, stiff. A little patch in front of me catches fire and from the burning grass, the voice repeats itself, 'Pfeffer . . . !' "

A pin jabbed the Shammos's cheek. Startled, he looked down. Heschele stared at him from the end of the table, an ugly sneer on his face. Mockingly, the little boy stuck out his tongue. The Shammos was astounded. Nevertheless he stammered out the end of the tale. " 'Pfeffer!' the voice says, 'Go west!' " Cruel and derisive laughter burst from the bottom of the table. Pfeffer looked at his grandson. "You're full of . . ." the little boy screamed.

"You are a little no-gootnick, Mr. Heschele," shouted the Shammos, "and I'm going to break your neck!" He jumped up. An apple splattered on the wall behind him. Pfeffer pushed his chair aside and began to chase Heschele around the room.

Who should come running in? Lily! She ran up to Pfeffer and grabbed him. "Don't touch! Don't touch the little one. It's your fault. I heard. He's right, you're full of it." She backed Pfeffer into the corner. "I listened Monday, Tuesday, behind the door. You know nothing. A big fake!" From behind his mother, Heschele kicked the Shammos in the calf. Lily grabbed Pfeffer by the lapels and shook him. "You got the brains of a dog!"

Pfeffer fell on his knees and began to bark. He bared his teeth at Heschele. "Stop! Stop!" screamed Lily, kicking her father. "You crazy?"

The Shammos stood up. He looked at his daughter. Her eyes were glittering green with hatred. A queen of Sodom. Pfeffer spat in her eye. He caught her wrist and spat again. He turned and walked out of the house. He never spoke to her again.

Ten days later the cops brought him home. After that the old men took care of him. One of the regulars at the G&G would take him by the arm and lead him to Lily's on Lorne Street, walk up the stairs with him to the second landing and knock on the door. Pfeffer slept in his old bed. He left the house every morning before his daughter woke up. They met once a month when his old-age pension arrived. Half of it she took for rent. So he had enough for coffee and a few bagles during the month. She could take it all. Pfeffer didn't care. He was through with life. He lived in dreams.

CHAPTER IX

The Master Electrician

SMILING, SHAMMOS Yossel Finklestein advanced. He walked down half the length of the G&G, greeting his parishioner with the big hello. "Pfeffer!" he shouted, "it's time for afternoon services, up!"

Mr. Pfeffer stared at Finklestein. "Mr. Pfeffer," said the Shammos, beaming, "I am glad to see you." He leaned over and pinched the Aroostook's cheek affectionately. "Up, Pfeffer, in a little while is minchah," said the Shammos, pushing the table to the side. He took Pfeffer gently by the lapels and yanked him out of his seat. Standing the Maine Shammos on his feet, Finklestein clapped his hands. "Time to go!" Pfeffer nodded. Finklestein turned and started for the door. Pfeffer followed after like a dog.

A face from the window stared at them, terrible to see. A pathetic face, sodden with grief. Squashed against the glass, looking in, filled with tears, blotched with pain. It peered into the delicatessen window, looking for a friend. It blinked with the neon sign in the window, aching with misery, distorted with hope. It foundered on the wet glass. Those who saw it had a hard time digesting their corned-beef sandwiches. A face like that is no hors d'oeuvre.

The Shammos recognized it. "Fagle!" he shouted, rushing toward the door.

Behind the glass the face burst with light. Brilliant, it flashed for a second, then went black as a worn-out bulb.

The face in the window belongs to Fagle, Isadore Fagle, master electrician, who never knew, before his fiftieth birthday, a taste of acid in the stomach. A man may live to a hundred and not see grief. It abides silent in him. He may come upon it as a young man, leave it behind. Or it may rise in the ripeness of age, as to Job, strike him, pull out the tent pegs, bring down the house—until he has to howl. Isadore! Tragedy flooded his life like a huge searchlight, drove him up and down the corridors where he had slept peacefully in the dark.

Why didn't experience prepare Mr. Fagle? Nothing in the first fifty years of his life indicated the disaster that was to overtake him. He went off to war and came back. A shell had hit him and left a few scratches. What's that? He traded a bone for a silver plate. It was only a nuisance. For physical discomforts he was prepared. Touch him with leprosy, he would have shrugged. Grief, discovering him, had to prepare a cunning snare.

Fagle grew up in Dorchester, the son of a candlemaker. Despite the electric light, religious candles did a good business. Sabbath candles were not replaced by Sabbath electric bulbs. In Dorchester, candlemaking remained a business. Old Mr. Fagle didn't make fortunes. But young Fagle didn't lack for anything special.

He went to high school. He went to war (No. 1). He came home. His father says, "I made with the candles. You make with the bulbs." So he makes with the bulbs. He became an electrician.

He got married. A girl with a father like old Fagle, a girl whose father says, "Your mother made with me. You make with someone else." So she made with Fagle. They were married. They lived. What else can one say? He became a master electrician. She became a good housewife. Children they didn't have. For twenty-five years they lived. Then she died.

On his fiftieth birthday Fagle found himself alone. Alone in a big house without a wife. Can a married man live alone? Fagle sat like a lump among his furniture, dishes, television and phonograph. His appliances went dead. After work he sat in the kitchen and stared at the stove. His work began to suffer. He fumbled with switches, screwed the bulbs in backward. One day he almost electrocuted himself in the wiring system of a Chinese laundry.

A friend took him aside. "Fagle, you got to go out! Make with the social life." So Fagle makes with the social life. He stumbles over to Hecht House, our community center, and takes out a card in the Golden Age Club.

The Golden Age Club! A solemn chord strikes in the imagination. In a dusty room filled with bookcases and fading prints, a small group of elders gathers in the shadows of afternoon to reminisce. The shouts of the marketplace are stilled. Quietly they recall among themselves the memories of an active life. Sports are not unknown. Exercise still helps the failing frame. On a sunny day a few go out to play croquet. The Ping-Pong table is dusted off. There are the trips: a bus ride to Concord and the nursery of Louisa May Alcott; a concert of bassoon and three-stringed clavichord music at the Jack Gardner Palace; the jaunts to a museum of stuffed wildlife in Boston.

One must be careful, however, about expending energy. Most afternoons would find the Golden Age Club seated quietly around the card tables in their room. Bridge and Whist are favored. Other games, though, Parchisi and Monopoly, provide diversion. Once a month, a wicked game of Canasta is got up.

Fagle walked into the room of the Golden Age Club at Hecht House. It was blinding pink. The walls had just been painted. A mob of screaming old ladies and men were gathered around a radio that was blaring out the results of the races at Suffolk Downs. At the far corner of the room old Menshick, the Golden Age book, was already paying off the receipts of the morning's numbers racket. The winning number was up on the wall, scotch-taped to the glass over Theodore Herzl's picture.

In the middle of the floor the rug had been pushed away and about fifteen people were trying to learn the Bunny Hop to a record that was shouting out on the phonograph over the track results. An old lady of eighty grabbed Fagle by the arm. "What?" he asked. She pointed to the wall, where a sign of crepe paper read, "Bunny Hop Dec. 8" and, pushing him into the circle began to hop up and down. Fagle turned to protest, but she pinched his buttock. He hopped.

He hopped right out of the circle and made for the door. A strong arm grabbed him as he stepped over the threshold. Shaindele Katz, hostess of the Golden Age, had him.

"Where are you going, bubbele?" Shaindele said sweetly, yanking Fagle back into the room. "Come on, have a cup of tea with me."

She hauled him across the floor to a chair, pushed him down into it and, before he could get up again, was back with a cup of tea.

"Excuse me," she said, spilling the tea in his lap. Fagle screamed. She had scalded his groin.

"Well, you made a mess," Shaindele said forbearingly. "So what, we'll clean it up."

She yanked his hand out from between his legs and, pulling him up, took him off to the ladies' room, where she applied Borax and water, ruining his pants forever. On the trip to the ladies' room, Shaindele found out about Fagle, his house, his television, his appliances, furniture, dishes, phonograph and some money in the bank.

Now who was Shaindele? Shaindele, Mrs. Shaindele Katz, had been the wife of Malcolm Katz, the coal man. Malcolm Katz had been a widower, age forty, when he married Shaindele. He had a fist the size of a pumpkin and a brain the size of a pea. Both were of use with Mrs. Katz. When he understood what she was saying to him, he gave her a good belt in the mouth. Most of the time he didn't understand. It went over his head and he couldn't pay any attention. All day he shoveled coal. He came home at night, fell into bed and slept. In the morning he got up, went off and shoveled coal. On weekends he drove off with his friends, the teamsters, to New York or Maine. Shaindele? In thirty years of marriage he shoveled eight children into her. What more could a good coal man do? At the age of seventy Malcolm Katz still had a brain the size of a pea, but his fist had shriveled to a tomato. Someone pushed him down the stairs. He died. He lay at the bottom of the stairs in his house like a sack of dry husks. Mrs. Katz looked down from the top of the stairs. She was fifty-five. She felt ripe. It was time for some planting.

All the time Malcolm Katz was out shoveling coal or pinching girls with the teamsters, his wife was not idle. She didn't sit at home with her eight children like an empty coal bin waiting to be filled. She was out finagling. She finagled in the politics, the organizations, the synagogues, of Dorchester. She appointed herself as the extra member of every committee and looked for a chance to make noise. Shaindele Katz and Daniel Dropnick, the funeral director, were the biggest troublemakers in Dorchester. In time they became cohorts. Whomever Dan couldn't threaten with his gangsters or buy off with a free Passover basket, Shaindele did away with with her tongue. For a ten-dollar bill, Shaindele could do a character assassination second only to Senator McCarthy.

After the death of her husband, Shaindele turned from troublemaking. She became a terror. She was everywhere, doing nothing. Heaven forbid, you didn't invite her to your party, function or political meeting. Up and down the length of Dorchester you were a dirty word. She stopped people on the Avenue, in the delicatessens, at synagogue, to tell them. And your wife? Who can command the adjectives that came out of Mrs. Katz's mouth?

When the Almighty was creating the world, when every phrase was Law, when "Let there be light" meant Light, the Devil whispered into the ear of God, "Let there be a Shaindele."

"A Shaindele!" Amazed, God muttered into his beard. "Let there be a Shaindele? Who ever heard of such a thing? Are you crazy?" He shouted at the Devil.

Too late! The Shaindeles of this world were already created. Inadvertently, God had spoken. All the Almighty could do was to curse them. He cursed them with His own big mouth.

Did Fagle know about Mrs. Shaindele Katz? He knew from nothing. He was ignorant as Job.

On the way to the ladies' room, when she found out about that small sum of money in the bank, Mrs. Katz began to think about marriage. Scrubbing Fagle's pants with Borax and water, she made up her mind. She whacked him in the thigh with the brush and asked, "You got a tootsie?"

Wedged in between two sinks, Fagle wasn't quite sure what she meant, but he shook his head. "Tommorrow at eight, pick me up!" Mrs. Katz commanded.

Mr. Fagle's heart leapt. He was frightened. He wasn't used to such a woman. He was going to say no. Then he thought, "Fagle! What's the matter? This is the social life. You came to make with it. So? *Make* with it."

"We'll go to the movies," purred Mrs. Katz like a kitten. Well, not exactly a kitten.

So for the next two weeks Fagle picked up Mrs. Katz at eight and the two of them went to the movies. When they finished with the two theaters in Dorchester, they went out in Fagle's pickup to the ritzy drive-ins of Brookline and Newton. Fagle would pick up a few boxes of potato chips and several gallons of orange soda in addition to Shaindele. Mrs. Katz sat contentedly in the front seat of the pickup, guzzling and chewing, one eye on the movie, the other on Fagle.

The first weekend they had a picnic in Franklin Field. Fagle stopped at the G&G beforehand and got a dozen corned-beef sandwiches. Also, at Mrs. Katz's request, he brought his bankbook, a copy of the deed to the house and a list of furniture and appliances. On the grass of Franklin Field, or rather the frosty ground (it was December), Fagle spread out the papers. Shaindele burped approvingly. A chill went through Mr. Fagle's legs.

The next weekend they spent at the Franklin Park Zoo. Mrs. Katz spent an hour and a half in front of the lions' cage. She fed them peanuts. She watched an old, bloated female lion stalk up and down the cage. The lioness dragged her enormous tongue along the floor of the pen, so that the peanuts just rolled into her mouth without effort.

"That's an animal!" thought Mrs. Katz. She could have hugged the old bitch.

Fagle had wandered away to the monkey cage. Shaindele caught up with him. She proposed.

The GOLDEN AGE CLUB of Dorchester begs to announce its Winter BUNNY HOP also a main attraction its No. 1 Hostess MRS. SHAINDELE KATZ is getting married there to Isadore Fagle. BE THERE ON TIME! TICKETS $2.50 at Door. December 8, 8:30 sharp.

Dorchester has never seen such a thing. A wedding! The service was performed downstairs in the gymnasium. The steam room was too small. Shaindele was a member of the Monday Night Calorie Club. She had free use of all athletic facilities. They hung the marriage canopy from a basketball net. The punching bags were wreathed with dandelions. Still, a gym smells like a gym. There was sweat in the air all through the ceremony. Overhead, people were tramping in for the dance. Bernie Schloffman's band was tuning up. As soon as the glass was broken, Shaindele hurried upstairs to the bunny hop. Fagle and the rest of the guests followed.

Everybody in Dorchester had been invited. Shaindele persuaded the Golden Age Club to send out twenty-five thousand invitations. It was like a political mailing. The Chelsea Golden Age got hold of one and showed up with total registration. Not an elected official in Dorchester who didn't stick his head in Hecht House. Of course, they went in one door and out the other. But each one stopped long enough at the main table to shake Mr. Fagle's hand and let Mrs. Fagle know that they had been there. However, there was no shortage of personages. A large number of bums and ward heelers sneaked in by way of the fire escape, waving invitations, and couldn't be ejected. Everyone who ever wore a button at the polls showed up for a free drink. At the far end of the room a rock-and-roll band banged and stomped. The daughters of Eire in South Boston sent fifty gray-haired colleens to jig. The crush was terrible. Several old ladies had to be removed to the Beth Israel by ambulance—heat prostration. In the middle of December!

Mrs. Shaindele Fagle was jumping up and down in the middle of the crowd, hopping, jigging, rhumba-ing. She even got down and did a kazahtzkah. A telegram had arrived with congratulations from the local congressman. Shaindele saw herself sitting on the State Democratic Committee. Maybe even the national one. President Johnson stops by.

"Listen, Lyndon, that shicksa gives you to eat nothing. Have a bagel." Shaindele could feel herself giving him a pinch on the cheek.

Fagle sat at the main table all through the evening behind a plate of green pickled tomatoes, pale as ghosts. He stirred an unfinished bowl of noodle soup. Beside him lay a pile of papers: his bank account, his deed to the house and the title to the furniture and pickup truck. They had all been signed over to Shaindele in a lawyer's office the day before. He watched his new wife barreling back and forth among the guests.

Maybe she would quiet down after the marriage. Certainly he, Fagle, was leading a more active life. A friend came up to him.

"Well, you are making with the social whirl!"

"Yeh," said Fagle.

Around midnight, when the last of the paying guests came through the door, Mrs. Shaindele Fagle decided it was time to leave. She went up to the main table, got hold of Mr. Fagle and marched toward the door. Menshick was totaling up the receipts at a table there.

"So what we got?" Shaindele asked, snatching the green money box out of the bookie's hands.

"The Golden Age Club made about ten thousand bucks," replied Menshick, trying to grab the box back.

"What do you mean, made the Golden Age? Is it your wedding or mine?" shouted Shaindele. She emptied the receipts into her pocketbook. "Bill me for expenses." And she tipped the table over, so that it fell back on old Menshick. He was pinned to the wall.

"Where!" he gasped.

"Florida," she replied, sailing out the door.

The next morning they flew to Miami. Reservations had been made at the Fountainebleau. Fifty dollars a day. Who made them? Mrs. Fagle looked at the chandeliers, the gilt on the walls, the rich carpets and the five potted palms in the lobby.

"This is the place," she said.

Mr. Fagle looked at the wiring in his room. "A cheap job," he thought.

All afternoon Shaindele lay on the beach. Her body tanned fast. She looked like a soft lump of brown sugar.

Mr. Fagle stayed under the umbrella. His skin became raw and red under the sun. Patches of it were always peeling off. He was left like a bleeding flounder. Occasionally Mrs. Fagle splashed and swam in the tepid waters. Mr. Fagle huddled miserably under the umbrella, trying to read magazines.

In the mornings Shaindele went shopping. It made Fagle sick when he heard the prices.

"You need a mink stole in Miami?" he burst out finally at the furrier's.

"Shut up!" said Mrs. Fagle. She turned to the owner of the store. "Don't pay no attention. I'll take it."

After that Fagle stayed home in the mornings. One day on the beach he found a friend from Dorchester, an old cigar salesman, retired. The friend played pinochle. So did Fagle. They found two others, and Fagle began to enjoy his mornings. When Mrs. Fagle went out the door, Fagle got on the phone and his friends came up.

If it wasn't for the evenings, things might have stayed quiet for a while. In the evenings Mrs. Fagle went out to dance. She needed a partner, Mr. Fagle went with her.

"I don't dance!" he began as she pulled him out of his chair when the rhumba began.

"Dance!" she commanded and, grabbing him into her fleshy arms, pushed out onto the dance floor with Fagle.

He stumbled, tripped, fell. When he twisted his ankle, Shaindele gave up.

"Tomorrow morning, you go to the dance class at Murray's, hear!"

"I'm not a dancer," Fagle protested.

"Hear!" Mrs. Fagle shouted. "Or else."

So began the mornings of misery. You know some people are born with talent in their legs, others in their hands. In the old days, when people chased each other around the world, throwing sticks and stones, there was a high price for a man with talent in his legs. It takes fancy footwork to outfox a lion. Nowadays, the premium seems to be on fellows with good hands. Is it because the hands are closer to the brain? In particular work, they do better. Shaindele's fox trot wouldn't help her screw in one of Mr. Fagle's sockets. Those big toes that thumped up and down instinctively to the rhumba —could they have spliced? Could they have wired? This did not console Mr. Fagle. He had a problem with the legs. Every morning they humiliated him at Murray's dance studio.

Each instructor in Murray's took him on. No one could help. Mr. Fagle wasn't a clumsy man. But when he started out on the floor something happened. He had danced before. All right, he wasn't Fred Astaire. Yet he could distinguish his right foot from his left. He marched in the Army. At the Jewish War Veterans' Dance once a year, he and his first wife did as well as any other couple. Like most of us, he could stumble along when the music began.

A devil took possession of him at Murray's. The loudspeaker announced, "One step forward."

Fagle stepped back.

"One step to the left."

Fagle stepped right. He cursed under his breath. Something was pushing him. Anger made his body tremble. The music began on the phonograph; his feet slid away. They went in all directions. They melted away, saying, "Sit on your toches. That's where your brains are. Use them!"

Fagle fell down. He got up on his knees. He crawled around on the floor, banging with his kneecaps. It wasn't the fox trot. One of the dance instructors ran over to help.

Fagle started shouting, "I'm trying! I'm trying!" He grabbed the instructor by the pants. "I haven't got three legs!"

Murray's man backed away. His pants, knotted in Fagle's grip, ripped. A long, hairy leg jutted out of a slit in the sleek black tuxedo pants. The ladies giggled; Fagle cursed his wife.

Finally, they let him sit in the corner. Mr. Fagle sat every morning at Murray's, twiddling his thumbs. A circuiting system buzzed in his head. It would electrocute everyone at Murray's.

However, Fagle won a consolation prize. Shaindele no longer demanded that he accompany her to evening dances. The pinochle games were switched to the night hours. There, among his three friends, Fagle could freely weep over his misfortunes.

Shaindele had found another partner. One afternoon in the water she met a Mr. Mendell. She was coming up from under the waves, after holding her breath for two

minutes on the sandy bottom. Mr. Mendell was swim-
ming overhead. Her huge head struck him square in the
belly. As she surfaced, Shaindele saw a man going
under, choking. In five feet of water she rescued him.
Mr. Mendell was five feet and two inches tall. So who
knows? He might have drowned.

On the beach, Shaindele banged on Mendell's stomach till the water came spurting out his mouth. Mendell came to in a hurry. He sat up on the Florida sands
and introduced himself.

"Jacob Mendell, my dear lady. I am in debt to you
for life."

It turned out he was a big realtor, a Tampa hotelman. Mrs. Fagle immediately made a date for coffee
the next morning.

It was love at first sight. Five foot two, eyes of blue,
Mr. Mendell stepped through the restaurant. In his
blue pinstripe suit, he looked like a banker. Shaindele
wanted to "kootchy-koo" him on the spot. Mr. Mendell's tanned, handsome face shone with the rosy glow
of a superb old age. There were still threads of black in
his gray hair, like narrow pin stripes. He looked like
one of the French Rothschilds, dapper but distinguished. A tiny mustache flicked out under his aquiline
nose, a touch of the devil.

Mrs. Fagle took the mink stole off the back of her
chair and threw it around her shoulders. She slumped
back in her seat like the Empress of Russia. To hide her
feelings, she shouted across half a dozen tables to the
advancing figure, "Mendell, bum, you're late!"

Mr. Mendell smiled as if she had paid him a charming compliment. He went up to her and kissed her hand. "My savior," he whispered into her ear, tickling it with his mustache. Then he looked at the clock, seated himself opposite her and said, "I'm early."

They talked for two hours. Mrs. Fagle went on and on about her political position in Boston, her recent rise to financial power. The mink around her shoulders, the diamond glittering on her finger, the expensive dress she wore—all made it credible.

Mr. Mendell began to elaborate about himself. He was building a new hotel, a little bigger than the New York Hilton. It was called The Flower of Tampa. Mrs. Fagle began to realize, as he talked, that Mendell was building not a hotel but an institution. It loomed like the Temple of Solomon in magnitude, the Hanging Gardens of Babylon in beauty.

"You speak about political power in Boston, my dear lady," said Mr. Mendell. "From The Flower of Tampa lobby will be wielded our industrial destiny in South America. Already, I and my friends . . ." Here he broke off, blushing. "I have been immodest," he said. Suddenly he looked up at the clock. "Oh, the time!" he exclaimed, rising. "Tonight, you are my guest at the Civic Ball. At the door we meet!" he called, threading through the tables.

Mrs. Fagle gaped open-mouthed after him. The waiter brought the check. She stared at the door, her tongue out.

He met her at the door. They slipped in through a side entrance.

"A friend of the Mayor!" Mendell confided to the cop. He flashed a little card.

They were inside. Mr. Mendell flew around Mrs. Fagle on tiptoes. He flawlessly executed the rhumba, the merengue, the bossa nova, and the cha-cha-cha. She was dazzled. Her heavy bosoms heaved under the brocade shimmer of her gold ball dress. They rumbled and tumbled under Mr. Mendell's quick eye like giant tender bowling balls. She let him get a good look, then swung around and showed her backside with a furious shake of the lindy. Mr. Mendell spread his hands a few feet away. He was like an explorer exulting over the globe. His eyes dilated with ecstasy as it revolved before him.

"What are the prospects?" Shaindele asked, turning back to him.

"Enormous," said the little man.

They danced every night that week.

"Ah, Shaindele, you make me feel young again!" exclaimed Mr. Mendell.

"And you, me," she responded.

He bit her ear lobe as they turned in a tango. She squeezed his cheek.

That evening, instead of saying good-bye to her in the lobby of the Fountainebleau, Mr. Mendell accompanied Shaindele to the door of her room.

"Before you go in, I want to tell you something, darling," said Mendell.

Mrs. Fagle bent down to hear. Mendell reached up, touched her lips and started shmootzing. When Shaindele realized what he was up to, she opened her mouth and almost popped his head inside. That was *her* way of shmootzing.

Mr. Fagle opened the door.

"What's going on?" he shouted. He yanked Mendell's head out of Shaindele's mouth. "You a dentist? This is my wife!"

Grabbing the hotelman by the collar, he ran down the corridor with him, then stopped and pushed him up against the wall.

"Fool around with my wife, I'll beat your brains out!"

Fagle let go of Mendell's collar and the little man collapsed on the floor of the corridor. As soon as Fagle turned back toward his door, Mr. Mendell began crawling toward the elevator. Fagle went up to Shaindele, who was standing by the door.

"Who are you? Mrs. Number One Call Girl?"

Shaindele was stunned. She was caught unprepared. She went to bed speechless.

The next morning, she recovered. "All right, bum," she said. "Tonight, *you* take me dancing."

"I'll be there!" Fagle shouted.

Shaindele was furious. She hadn't intended to be taken up on the invitation. She already had a date that night with Mr. Mendell. All day she stalked around the room, scratching the furniture with her nails. Finally she went out and bought a new dress. Fagle had gone off to Murray's to practice.

That night Mr. and Mrs. Fagle arrived together at the Civic Ball. Mrs. Fagle was tricked out from head to toe: a dress of green satin, a white ermine stole, an enormous coiffure rising two feet off her head, blonde hair set with strings of rhinestones, crowned with a gold tiara. She was beguiling.

Mr. Fagle was trembling. Every bone in his body shook with anger, even the silver plate. He was wearing a black wedding tuxedo stained with noodle soup. They marched together to the center of the dance floor. The band struck up a cha-cha-cha.

"All right, smartie, dance!" commanded Mrs. Fagle.

She grabbed his left shoulder with one gloved hand. With her other she pushed his right arm into the air. They clasped hands in a tight fist.

"Cha-cha-cha!" barked Mrs. Fagle.

"You watch!" shouted Fagle. He pushed her to the right. He pushed her to the left. Back and forth he yanked Shaindele, crying, "Cha-cha-cha, cha-cha-cha."

His legs began to melt under him. Jumping up into the air, Fagle came down on Shaindele's foot. "Cha-cha-cha!" he shouted in her face. He tumbled between her skirts on the hardwood floor. He wept, banging his fists.

"Bum!" Mrs. Fagle was screaming, hopping, holding her injured foot in the air. She kicked the prostrate body of her husband. "A wooden leg you got!" She kicked him in the calf. "A leg of wood!"

Mr. Mendell slid out of the crowd around Mr. and Mrs. Fagle. He sneaked up behind Shaindele's ear and whispered, "This dance, might I have the pleasure?"

Shaindele turned. "It's mine, the pleasure!" She took his arm and started into the crowd.

Fagle jumped up. "It's silver!" he shouted at her back. He pulled up his trouser leg. A long scar gaped, shrapnel 1918. The scar was bleeding. "It's a silver leg I got!" he screamed at the crowd.

Shaindele and Mr. Mendell had disappeared.

Two hours later Mr. Fagle was packed. He took a taxi to the airport and got the first plane that left for Boston.

Mrs. Fagle had wired ahead to her children:

THE BUM IS COMING STOP LOCK HIM OUT

Mr. Fagle arrived in Dorchester. He walked up the steps to his house. The key didn't fit. The lock in the door was changed. He went around to the front window. It was shut tight. Fagle picked up a stone. He would break the glass and push the lock back, then push up the frame and get in. A man appeared at the window. It was Shaindele's oldest son, Charlie.

He opened the window and shouted out, "Get away, Fagle!"

"What do you mean, get away?" said Fagle. "It's my house!"

"No more," said Charlie. He brandished a coal shovel in Fagle's face. "You heard, no more!"

Fagle threw the stone. It caught Charlie on the nose; blood popped out in the stream. With the shovel, Charlie smashed Fagle on the head. This Charlie was a garbage man, built like the father. He smashed, it wasn't funny. Fagle lay on the ground, out cold. An ambulance took him away.

The next day Fagle went to the lawyers. What could

they do? Mr. Fagle could hardly talk. His head was wrapped with bandages. His eyes were so full of tears, he couldn't see straight. He was delirious. He became more so.

"It's an airtight deed she drew up on you," the lawyers told him. "The house is hers! You signed."

Fagle went from lawyer to lawyer. No one wanted the case. There wasn't a judge in Dorchester anxious to be on the bad side of Shaindele.

Shaindele Fagle arrived back in Dorchester. It seems that Mr. Mendell's hotel was only in the planning stage. Plans take money. Mrs. Fagle wasn't ready to invest in plans.

"It's a nice place," she said, looking at the empty lot in the middle of Tampa with him.

"A few hundred thousand would get the ball rolling," said Mr. Mendell, flashing his handsome smile.

"Yeah," said Mrs. Fagle. She took the next bus back to Miami.

A bill waited for her at the desk in the lobby of the Fountainebleau. She looked in her bankbook and decided to board the afternoon plane for Boston.

Mr. Fagle went to see his wife. He knocked on the door of his house. "I want to make . . ."

She slammed it in his face. He telephoned. She hung up. He sent letters. No answer came back. He waited in the street outside the house. She called the cops and had him chased away. At the Golden Age Club he was declared *persona non grata*. He haunted the delicatessens, hoping to meet her. She didn't even come in for a pickle. He went to see the Rabbi. The Rabbi called.

The Rabbi mentioned Mr. Fagle. Shaindele began to
yell. The Rabbi held the receiver away from his ear.
Fagle could hear the dirty words being shouted.

Fagle had rented a room in a house on Blue Hill
Avenue. All night he lay awake weeping. His work
began to suffer. He was hired to wire a downtown Boston hotel. He wept into the circuits. Upon request of
the hotel management and the Fire Department, the
union had to remove him from the job. Not, however,
before he had short-circuited the neon sign outside. It
went up in flames just as he was leaving.

The union found him another job. He was a member
in good standing for over forty years. He was a veteran
of World War I. He always voted Democratic. It was
time for them to do a favor for Fagle. One of their little
plums, the fruit of political patronage, was secured for
him. He was installed as master electrician in the
Dewey Square Underpass. A good job, a steady income,
favorable working conditions! What was required? At
six in the evening Fagle showed up and flicked the
lights on. At six in the morning Fagle made another
appearance and flicked the lights off. Simple? A single
switch did the trick. Fagle showed up at six in the evening. He was weeping. Tears were streaming from his
eyes. He could hardly see straight. He flicked the lights
off. At six in the morning, he showed up again, still
crying, and flicked the lights on.

This was the end of Mr. Fagle's employment as an
electrician. He went back to his room on Blue Hill
Avenue with a bottle and started drinking. He wept
and drank, day after day, till his clothes were soaked in

alcohol and tears. He staggered out onto the Avenue, stopping people in the street, trying to tell them his troubles. He started with his leg, pulling up the trouser, showing them the scar, crying about it. He went on to his first wife, her death, the empty house. Then he began on Shaindele Katz. He howled. Up and down Blue Hill Avenue, howling what this wife had done; in the back seats of synagogues, in the delicatessens, from table to table, he wept and called her names.

The community laughed at him. Tell them something new. Shaindele had had a dirty name for years.

Fagle started screaming. A short circuit in his head. "Switch it off! Switch it off!" No one would listen in the G&G.

Until the lights went out. Every one. Someone unscrewed the switch at midnight, the busiest hour of our delicatessens. They had to slice corned-beef sandwiches in pitch black. Vey iz mir! How many fingers were lost? And the customers stumbled over one another, trying to get out the door in the dark. "Switch it on! Switch it on!"

"What should I do? What should I do?" cried Fagle. The community yawned at the tables.

Then someone monkeyed with the telephone wires. In the dead of night a phantom climbed poles all over Dorchester, splicing, cutting, hooking, unhooking, plugging in and out. In the morning the lines from Roxbury to Mattapan were all tangled. A mess! At seven A.M. the Litvasher Rabbi of Dorchester picked up his phone to call a synagogue in Newton. He was anxious to get a plush seat as Rabbi there. A touchy man

who never forgave an insult, he wasn't getting along
with his quarrelsome congregation. And who has been
spliced into his private line but a close friend, the
Galitzianer of Roxbury, the Tsaddik of Lawrence Avenue. A man who is up early too, talking to the president
of the very synagogue in Newton that the Litvasher
was in the act of dialing. ". . . a dope . . . the Litvasher?
. . . A nincompoop . . . doesn't know his Hebrew . . .
steals from the synagogue . . . not for you . . . picks his
nose all through the service!" Not only did the Litvasher's ears prick up, but so did those of three or four
board members of his schul in Dorchester, who had
been cut into this private line.

At eight A.M. the politicians were up, pulling deals.
They had all been hooked up on a party line. One over-
heard the other. "That shmock . . . Senator Plotz—a
bookie?"

"Four months in the Nut House?"

"A queer!"

"For *you* he'll vote? He took from me. You're washed
up, he told *me!*"

"On the records, check for yourself!"

"He'll wake up this morning . . ."

"A faker of the highest order. A parasite."

"It'll be gone. Look high and low. You won't find
it."

"Nothin'. A knife in his back. They're gettin' ready to
dump him in Boston Bay."

"At the window? Already? Does he see his car?"

"Rigged? I'm telling you. I'M gonna be standin' in
the votin' machine."

"For ten thousand he sold it?"

"Five thousand!"

"Hello?"

"Hello!"

At nine A.M. their colleagues, the lawyers, started calling and listening to fee cutting, client stealing and mutual defamation. Soon the bakers, the cleaners, the druggists, were on one another's phones. Neighbors were plugged into each other's lives. Husbands in downtown Boston offices picked up their receivers and heard their wives at home on the phone with boy friends. By twelve o'clock all was silence on the wires of Dorchester. No one could talk on the telephone. They had to meet in the streets. Small groups milled on the Avenue. There were shouts of outrage. Was there a Devil in the midst of the community? What should they do? What should they do?

People were angry with one another. Irritable. In a mood to believe anything.

Fagle lay in his room, a pillar of fire in his brain. He saw Mrs. Fagle, her mammoth white thighs, naked, lying back on the bed in his house. Outside the door a line of men—truck drivers, hackies, garbage men— laughed and joked, waiting for a turn at her. She was running a brothel. Dirty and smelling of sweat, they sat in his kitchen, telling gross stories, throwing beer cans at his clean cream walls. They wandered through the bedrooms, urinating at will. Opening the door to the bedroom, they hooted encouragement as Shaindele began to lie with two or three at a time. She lay back in the bed laughing, grunting like a hippo.

Fagle jumped up and pulled the plug out of his dream. The liquor stank in his breath. It was no dream! No! No! He hurried down to the G&G to tell people.

No one before had paid any attention to his story. It was the truth. Everyone knew it. What he spoke about now was fantastic. The tale had an appeal.

This was real slander. Better even than Shaindele's. His wife was running a brothel? Yes! Yes! In tears he told them, names too. So and so from the linoleum store. You know who of the Chinese laundry. I don't have to tell you from the bakery on Whatchmacallit Street. The stories spread faster than usual through the special agency of all Shaindele's victims. People went a bit crazy. They substituted one another's names for those Fagle had given them. Half of Dorchester was soon rumored to have been in Shaindele's bedroom. No one was safe. And then this got right back to Mrs. Fagle.

It happened that Shaindele had indeed been carrying on since her return. She was furious. Down to the G&G she hurried, to the New Yorker Delicatessen too, to every store and restaurant in Dorchester to stop the stories. What good was it? Fagle had preceded her. People were afraid to talk to her. They ran away. Who wanted to get a reputation? She almost blew a fuse.

What a sight! Shaindele standing in the middle of an empty delicatessen. With Fagle looking in—crying. Shedding tears over Fate.

CHAPTER X

The Drunk of Hosmer Street

SHAMMOS FINKLESTEIN met Fagle at the door. "Mr. Fagle, it's good to see you," he said.

The electrician fell weeping upon his neck. He sobbed into the damp wool suit of the Shammos. Finklestein pulled a handkerchief out of his pocket.

"Fagle, blow your nose," he suggested.

Fagle blew his nose. Pfeffer, the Aroostook Shammos, had come up behind them. He patted the electrician on the back. Mr. Fagle turned around, saw Mr. Pfeffer and fell on his neck, crying anew.

"My wife, my wife," he wept, "a killer!"

"Blow your nose, Fagle!" the Shammos ordered, taking him by the shoulder. "You'll feel better."

And it's true! There is nothing in the world like blowing your nose to clear your head. It does a world of good.

"Come on, boys," said the Shammos. "You'll go to services. It'll cheer you up, one hundred per cent. A half an hour is minchah. We got seven yet to get."

Shammos Finklestein looked up and down the Avenue. Which way to go to get? Didn't God speak to the prophets? He gave face to face directions to Moses. Jacob didn't have to go to a travel agency. They sent an angel to him in a dream. Shammos Yossel Finklestein was a religious leader too. He felt a faint stirring in his bones. Something tickled him in the right nostril. He turned that way and headed up the Avenue.

As the Shammos and his men made their way up the Avenue, a distant rumble descended the slope. It rolled down from behind the long wall of Franklin Field. There in the shade of the great stones lay a body. One of the strong men of Israel was felled in the grass, Muzzel the Drunk of Hosmer Street.

The sound which reached the Shammos's ears was distinct. It was a peal of thunder over the plain of Sharon. A familiar melody of the synagogue, it could be heard regularly every Saturday morning from the back benches of the schul. It was available any day of the week a Kiddush was announced in Dorchester, Mattapan or Roxbury. Occasionally it even took a trip on the trolley to Brookline. Let a bottle of liquor appear on the table for the repast after the service—and Muzzel the Drunk stepped through the synagogue doorway, a pious smile on his lips. Indeed, in deference to the feelings of the congregation, he would arrive early an hour and snore through the sermon. So when the blasts of the ram's horn rolled from behind the wall boulders, the heart of the Shammos bounded like a lamb. He knew it; the sleepy cry of the faithful.

"Hey, Muzzel, shlimuzzel, koom, up!" the Shammos barked.

On the other side of the wall, Muzzel blinked an eye. The sun moved with heat through the grass and tickled his red nose. The blade of a dandelion pricked the purple vein of his nostril. His head swam with the warmth of May and he twisted his sodden limbs up into the bale of fire. The grass, caught up in a hot breeze, brushed his face. It teased him. It touched him. The huge body of Muzzel writhed pleasurably in the grass. Through green blades and the gold strands of the sun a young woman's calves wheeled by after a baby carriage. He rubbed his cheek on the unshaven earth. Down the Avenue someone was calling someone a shlimuzzel. A young girl bobbed by in a blouse. The thighs of the Drunk ached pleasantly. He drew his legs together, curled himself up and turned back to sleep.

"Hey, Muzzel, shlimuzzel, koom, minchah!" the voice of the Shammos remonstrated harshly as he neared the wall. But Muzzel the Drunk of Hosmer Street dwelt now among the tents of the daughters of Canaan and the wine bags of their fathers. The Shammos shouted two or three times more. He reached the place in the wall opposite the snores. He banged his frail, bony fist on the stones. If Moses could draw water from a rock, he could draw one Jew for a minyan.

"Koom, koom!" he cried over the top of the wall. Its thick slabs towered four or five feet above the Shammos's head. Muzzel's snore echoed back in a lazy drone.

"Koom, koom!" the Shammos screamed. He wheeled on his companions and pointed to himself. "Koom, koom!" Understanding, they seized him, one to each skinny leg, and pushed from the rear. As they hoisted the Shammos, he ground the iron shank of his heel into the eye socket of one and, to maintain his balance, dug the toe of a cracked leather boot into the jaw of the other. As he sat back the disciples flung their master onto the top of the Franklin Field wall.

"Muzzel, Muzzel, minchah!" the Shammos wailed, rubbing his skinned buttocks. The Drunk slept as if the wax of the Cedars of Lebanon were poured in his ears.

The Shammos stopped rubbing his behind. He took his hand out and rubbed his forehead. What to do? Suddenly his lips pursed. He reached with his free hand into the pocket of the greatcoat and pulled out a bottle of gin. It was the tithe of Kaplan's liquor store to the Kiddush after minchah. Up and down he sloshed the silver liquid. It tinkled like a bell in the ear of the Drunk. Forthwith his head began to rise. His eyes opened. He saw the Shammos. And he smiled.

Ah, but the movement of his smile evoked more than the crude melody of words could ever hope to encompass. The smile of Muzzel the Drunk distilled the juice of a thousand Sunkist Florida oranges. It was in itself . . . a page from the Book of life. It was a mark of his innocence, his humility, his perpetual good humor. Nothing could disturb it. When the squad of Irish policemen arrived in their paddy wagon to dislodge him from the bar at Ye Little Browne Jug on Morton Street, he would weep with delight. "My friends, my friends, the Goyim," he laughed, climbing into their stocky blue arms. "You're always taking care of me. Come on, have a drink!" He grabbed the sergeant and kissed his beet-red face. "I couldn't do too much for you. You always got a place for me!" And he sang songs to them all the way to Station Nine.

For beauty of piety, the smile of Muzzel was un-
matched. During the Shira before the service he would
sit rapt in unthinking ecstasy as the Rabbi expounded
the Talmud. He caught every inflection of the teacher's
voice. And leaning back, he would stretch his bulky
shoulders, sighing with pleasure at the sound of so
much learning. Behind his enormous back the Orthodox scratched their beards and puzzled their yarmulkes
over Muzzel of Hosmer Street. How had he come
among the Jews? Who could explain among an abstemi-
ous people the appearance of such a drinker? In the
back of the synagogue some whispered that the Drunk
was a degenerate remnant of Canaan's tall people,
Rephaim and Anakim, the men of high stature, while
others claimed him for a son of Og of Basham, king of
the giants. But to the slander behind his broad neck,
Muzzel was deaf. When the Rabbi had finished his lesson, the Drunk was the first on his feet to congratulate
him. "Rabbi! What an interpretation! You make my
head ache. Better than Rashi!" And then he would
smile. What a smile! If Shammai had smiled on Hillel
with such a smile?

So even the Rabbi had to smile at him. Who could
scold a face with such a look? In the face of that child-
ish smile few even among the stony-hearted and tight-
pocketed of Blue Hill Avenue would not relent and give
him a finiff for a bottle.

His enormous bald head shone like a polished nut. It
was almost black from exposure, for he lay lolling in the
gutter for hours under the sun. Usually it hung down
sheepishly over his broad chest between two slack

jowls of smooth flesh as he averted his eyes from the derisive gaze of the community and searched instead along the sidewalk pavement for luck and treasure: a nickel, a dime, even a penny, maybe a half-smoked cigar, and sometimes in a great while the find of a half-pint bottle cast away with a little of the liquor yet remaining.

For though it seem empty (God's secrets were infinite) one might still partake of its essence in licking the film that stuck to the inside. Many times he had sat on the curb of the great thoroughfare of the Jews in America, Blue Hill Avenue, and broken the bottles. Their names were like poetry to him—Four Roses, Silk and Satin, Courvoisier . . . They reminded him of things, of situations, of people. *Three Monks* . . . as his thick tongue wandered harmlessly over the sweet, stinging edges of the fragments he contemplated the Christian mystery of three in one, one in three. Old Forester . . . he thought of America, its vast natural resources, the great redwood forests, the fortunes his brethren had made in California. Old Crow . . . he was reminded of his companion, Insoft the Cantor from Havana, driven by an ungrateful congregation from his remunerative position as the chief Cantor of Cuba after sacrificing his voice in the service of those no-gootnick Jews. Old Grand-Dad . . . and a sense of his own curse descended upon his shoulders . . . despised by his own children, and his children's children . . . driven from the house by a yente of a wife . . . forced to sleep on park benches. How that family demanding sustenance and support had sprung up, Muzzel could never quite comprehend.

To him it was enough to work now and then for a few dollars as a butcher's assistant. On a few dollars one could get drunk and loll contentedly in the gutter or fall asleep in the tall grass of Franklin Field. Muzzel led a pastoral life. Could one attribute blame to him in that he avoided returning home? To return to Hosmer Street and a flat full of crying children growing up under the tutelage of that forceful and sarcastic woman, his wife, to become the whores and hoodlums of Dorchester? To his face they screamed at him. On Blue Hill Avenue they cursed their own father to his face. And behind his back they disowned him. His children's children made a joke of him. Muzzel's eyes would water as his tongue flicked the last drop from the fragment of the Old Grand-Dad bottle. That his children should bring up their children that way. The state of the Jews was a terrible thing.

CHAPTER XI

Crash Ending

MUZZEL CAME up to the wall. His eyes rolled like a clown's with delight. The sun smeared gilt on his cheeks. His face lit up. He beamed as the bottle in the fingers of Shammos Yossel Finklestein swayed by its silver neck. "What you got for me?" he asked. His nose burned bright, red with enthusiasm.

"For you?" whispered Yossel. "For you?" Muzzel leaned forward to hear, laughing. He pointed his purple nostrils inquisitively toward the bottle. Shammos Yossel grabbed him by them. Seizing Muzzel's flaming nose, Finklestein hauled him to the top of the Franklin Field wall. "For you I got after," he said. The bottle dropped into the Shammos's pocket. He yanked the drunk by the arm and both of them jumped down onto the sidewalk.

Stunned by the sudden leap across the wall, Muzzel lay on the pavement. Liquor splashed in Finklestein's pocket. Muzzel came to. "When is after?" he asked, picking himself up.

The Shammos didn't hear him. He had scrambled to his feet a moment before and was striding up and down, smashing a fist into his palm. Right and left, down the Avenue he looked. No one. The shadows of afternoon were lengthening. They spread across the sidewalk, shrouding it. In the hollow heart of Shammos Finklestein they thronged, gray shapes of the past. They blew through its chambers like a dark wind. Breath, empty breath, took hold of him.

Finklestein coughed. He turned to his followers. "Where?" His eyes blazed. "Where?" Muzzel's smile slipped through his teeth and hung on the drunk's lower lip. Fagle hid in his handkerchief. Pfeffer tried to look the other way. "We got to get six!" shouted the Shammos. "What's happening? God is playing tricks?" He kicked the field wall. The Shammos was losing faith.

Hear, O Israel—a loud crash. Thunder! Lightning! A pillar of fire from the Heavens to Blue Hill Avenue.

No. Let us have strict truth. A voice that shook mountains from their bases; that caused the waters to swell and toss, fleeing from its wrath; that tore valleys into the earth: "What ails you, O sea, that you flee? You mountains, that you skip like rams?" Not quite. But a distant echo. Take what you get. It was loud. It was a crash.

A cascade of flowers erupted into the air. A black Cadillac bolted into the sky. The blare of horns sounded. A shout went up. Steel smashed against steel. Screams and groans. Showers of fruit and vegetables rained down. Over all soared a horse and junk wagon. The chariot of Elijah? What was up? The end of the world?

The Shammos and his men galloped toward the scene of the accident.

"The hills did tremble, and their carcasses were as

refuse in the street." Who has seen such a thing? People were running around screaming. Not those that were hurt. They sat still or lay where they were, biting their tongues with pain. The rest of the mob involved in the accident were up and about, howling bloody murder! "You did it!" they shouted, jumping out of their dented cars. They fell on the first fellow they saw and tried to smash him a good one before the cops came. "Crippled for life!" they screamed, banging each other with their fists. For the Shammos and his minyan they had no time. They were waiting for the insurance adjustors.

Finklestein and his boys wandered through this pavilion of flowers, scattered fruit and vegetables, wrecked automobiles and dented human beings, searching. You would think suffering would make people religious. No one was interested in joining a minyan. The Shammos wandered over rivers of gasoline and pools of blood, peeking under an M.T.A. bus and stopping a departing ambulance in his quest. He put his head in an ice cream locker and asked Dan Dropnick. Dan was out cold. Finklestein closed the ice cream locker. He came on Lennie the Shtup, lying in a casket filled with rotten tomatoes. Lennie didn't answer. Yossel felt the Bookie's forehead. His soul had fled. The Shammos was about to ask Heaven what was the use of all this bloodshed when he saw Max the Tax Kupperstein.

"Max!" he shouted. "This doesn't make you religious?" "Finklestein," Kupperstein shouted back, "I'm religious! You want converts? Take a look!" The taxi

driver pointed over the Shammos's shoulder. Yossel
turned around and looked across the car-strewn area.
At the edge of the wreckage, clear of the accident,
stood a junkman, Cantor, Moyhel and a Mshulach, with
their horse and wagon intact. The group rocked back
and forth in tears. Were they praying? Yossel grabbed
Max by the arm and rushed toward his friends. The
Junkman was cursing his horse. The Cantor was wailing in falsetto. The Moyhel scraped his nails on his
face. The Mshulach stamped up and down on a little
can. "Nu!" shouted Yossel. They recognized Finklestein. And they lifted their arms and let their anguish
be known to his Benefactor.

Yes, Druckman, Insoft, Dreizen and Tschernikoff
were safe and in tears. All the damage they had done
was spread out before them. They had caused it. What
had happened to them? Nothing.

> O Thou who art all-good, whose miracles
> never fail us.

Was it fair? Millions of dollars in torts they had created. Not a penny of it was for them. They were un-
touched. They had not a bruise on a kneecap. Oceans
of liability tossed before them. High and dry, they
thirsted for a drop. They were faint with need. Sam
Dropnick lay in an ice cream chest, good for a cool
$50,000. Even Lennie the Shtup could put in a claim.
Who needed the money? It was insane. What kind of
thing was God pulling? What was this supposed to
be—a miracle? A dirty trick!

They were in tears. "A scratch! My right arm for one!

One!" howled Insoft. "What's the trouble, boys?" shouted Shammos Yossel, coming up to the group around the junk wagon.

"Trouble? Who got trouble?" rasped Dreizen. "We are all in one hundred per cent health." He bit his lip and began to weep.

"Health is wealth," said Finklestein cheeringly. Tschernikoff lifted a can to hit him. "You boys need a little religious guidance," suggested the Shammos. "Come on to minchah!"

"At a time like this, how can you talk minchah?" snapped Druckman.

"Shame," said Dreizen.

"Who did this?" cried Insoft, shaking his finger at the Heavens. "He wants? He wants minchah? Answer! Let Him!"

A police siren tore through the air. "I wouldn't wanna be around to answer, Who did this?" said Max Kupperstein in a whisper. "Especially at a time like this. You could sit in jail for a hundred years for this. I'd find a cellar to sit in for a while and hide my head."

"A cellar?" asked Druckman. "You know a cellar?" Max looked at Finklestein.

"I know of a basement," said the Shammos. "A basement nobody has looked in for a long time."

"Minchah!" said Druckman.

"Let's go!"

"Ehhhhhh! Ehhhhh!"

"No? Who said? Heh?"

A chorus of voices responded. "Why not? Everyone scrambled into the wagon. Fagle, Pfeffer and Muzzel, who had come up from behind, were herded in too. "The sun is setting." "Not a moment to lose." "Late! Why? Let's not be!" Insoft hopped up and down. Shammos Yossel in the driver's seat smiled. This was how a pious congregation sounds.

So just ahead of the paddy wagon they galloped off down the Avenue. The cops never knew whether it was a phantom or not—what caused the accident. And to this day they see things when you mention the case at John Hancock.

Our wagon now draws to its destination. On the splintered floorboards between battered sides is borne a cargo, a minyan, to the impoverished basement of Young Israel. "Only ten men," you say? "What's that?"

Listen, God doesn't go in for numbers. He didn't choose the biggest tribe in the world. He took one man aside, Abraham, and said, "I'll do right by you!" You don't have to fill Madison Square Garden. Ten males above the age of thirteen—services start! It will suffice.

Suffice! Those ten souls borne in a broken junk wagon down Blue Hill Avenue are more precious, tastier than the grease of a bullock on the fire. God's nostrils fill with the sweetness of man's love. Now and then His methods for getting it are unorthodox. God is only human.

The wagon rolled to a stop in front of Young Israel. The Shammos jumped off. The old men piled out. One by one, Finklestein counted them: himself, Fagle, Pfeffer, Muzzel, Max, Druckman, Dreizen, Insoft, Tschernikoff . . . Oy! He started counting again, fast.

One, two, three, four, five, six, seven, eight, nine . . .
They were only nine. One he was missing. Missing!

Toward its berth in the horizon rushed the sun. A
police siren screamed on the Avenue. "I'm dying," said
Finklestein. The old men ran up the stairs to the door.
"Let us in!" shouted Druckman from the top. "You got
the key."

The Shammos clutched at his breast. His face
squeezed as if in a heart attack. He toppled headlong to
the street. "Vey," moaned the old men. They tumbled
down the stairs. In the gutter lay Shammos Yossel Finklestein on his back, staring up at the belly of a horse.

They were shocked. They were silent. Mr. Pfeffer
began to mumble. His lips moved quickly back and
forth. "Killed, killed," whispered Fagle. Druckman
coughed into his cap. The can of Mr. Tschernikoff
hung limp and soundless by his side. Max Kupperstein
and Muzzel leaned over the body while Mr. Dreizen
bent down to examine it. The Moyhel had looked many
times into the face of birth. Was this the face of death?

Above them Insoft began in a quiet voice to recite
the mourner's kaddish. In a bitter whisper, they all
joined him, "Yisgadal, v'yiskadash . . ."

Shammos Yossel Finklestein opened his eyes. He
looked at them. "I should only be dead," he said. Re-
proachfully he looked up. He screamed. Zei gesunt!
Over his eyes the Shammos clapped his hands. Who
could believe what he saw? The old men bent under
the belly of the horse. "There, a miracle!"

"A circumcised horse?" cried Insoft, standing up.

Dreizen the expert leaned under. "It's a genuine job," he affirmed. The congregation turned to Druckman. "Where did you pick this horse up?" asked Max. Mr. Druckman was scratching his bare head. In all the years he had the horse, Druckman had checked its teeth and its lips, combed its coat and looked at its hooves every other day. Yet not once had he come in contact with this fact. "I had him from the Shochet on Eire Street," replied the Junkman, dumbfounded. "The Shochet on Eire Street!" "A pious man!" "He must have done it!"

The ritual slaughterer on Eire Street in the opinion of our congregation had done the deed. It was remembered that the Shochet had lived a long life childless. He adopted a horse. He was zealous to leave a son. So he brought it into the faith.

"Is this horse over thirteen?" asked Shammos Yossel. "Older than me!" answered Druckman. "He's good for social security." "Well," said the Shammos, "it looks like we got a minyan."

So ten Jews climbed up the stairs of Young Israel of Dorchester. Nine members of the congregation marched through the door. The tenth got stuck in the doorway. "Whoah!" shouted Druckman. They backed their fellow member out onto the porch. How to get him into the tabernacle?

"It's all right," said the Shammos. "We are opening up our annex." Finklestein darted through the hall. He bolted down the stairs into the synagogue and grabbed the doorknob of the utility closet. Rushing to the window on Blue Hill Avenue, he threw it open and called, "Bring him over here! I got an A-1 seat."

So they sat the horse down on the little plot of dirt between the bushes and the window of the utility closet. They stuck his head through the open frame. They patted him on the toches and smiled to each other. They had done it right.

In a few minutes the solemn sound of prayer floats out the doorway of Young Israel. Bnai Tsurris has started its minchah service. At the window one of the members cranes his head forward, listening. His lips curl with pleasure. He swishes his tail and thinks, "The state of the Jews . . . ?"